Also by DJ Geribo

The House at the Top of the Trees
Eddie Easel and the Case of the Missing Green
The Miracle Dog
Mouse Bound
Seven Storied Houses
Me & Them
The Mart

All titles are available for purchase directly from BBD
Publishing at www.BBDPublishing.com.

Selected titles are also available on Amazon in paperback and
Kindle formats.

Deep Lake House

Deep Lake House

DJ GERIBO

BBD PUBLISHING ~ ALTON, NH

Deep Lake House is published by:

BBD Publishing
P.O. Box 351
Alton, NH 03809

www.BBDPublishing.com

Book layout and editing by James J. Fontaine

Cover design by Positively Creative Solutions, LLC

Printed in the United States of America

10 9 8 7 6 5 4 3 2 1

Library of Congress Control Number: 2024946289

ISBN 978-0-9883068-8-2

To Jim,

Who planted the tiniest seed in my brain for this one and I took off running in a different direction, into the arms of my muse.

TABLE OF CONTENTS

Chapter 1 - The House (Present Day) 1

Chapter 2 - Philip Donovan (1890s) 9

Chapter 3 - The Cohens (1920s) 17

Chapter 4 - Guy de Bourbon (1930s) 31

Chapter 5 - The Whitmores (1940s) 45

Chapter 6 - Miss Loretta (1940s) 53

Chapter 7 - Maisy Tuttle (1950s) 73

Chapter 8 - Mitchell Stewart (1950s) 87

Chapter 9 - Joanne and Drake (1970s) 109

Chapter 10 - The Boydins (1990s) 127

Special Acknowledgements 141

About the Author 143

Other Books by DJ Geribo 145

Leave Us a Review 149

The House

(Present Day)

Chapter 1

I am old. The paint in my rooms is peeling off the walls, the wallpaper is curling at the seams. My barnboard flooring is scuffed and worn from much walking and running with hard-soled shoes.

My shutters outside have all come off due to harsh winter snow and ice, fierce winds and rain, and feverishly baked summers. Time. Time has been the enemy. My days might be numbered. But there is always hope. I've been here twice before. And both times someone with a vision saw my potential and painted, repaired, tore down and built up my walls, and brought new life inside. Twice. But I'm at the point of structural damage and there is no rescuer in sight.

It has been a good life that I've had, some 210 years. And the stories I could tell. These walls do talk and I will share with whoever wants to listen. Some stories are sad and filled with pain and suffering, many are full of joy and bursting with love. I've seen hate and even a murder. And, of course, I heard there was a drowning or two in the lake. Beer bottles and champagne glasses have been thrown against my walls. There are even a couple of bullet holes. Laughter has echoed down my halls along with running and hand clapping. Joyous times and solemn ones. I witnessed extremes on both ends week after week, year after year, for decades and more.

When I was first built, life was quite simple. Materials weren't as durable as they are now. Newspapers lined inside my walls and served as insulation to try to keep Deep Lake House warm. Not many people came in the winter months, so the original owner closed the house up, which is why he had to sell; he couldn't afford the upkeep through the winter months with no guests staying. And then the Civil War in 1861-1865 kept people away for a few years, as well as WWI in 1914-18 and WWII in 1941-45. The second owner was a bit wealthier, so was able to add insulation and a better heating system to augment the fireplaces in each room to keep the House warm so it could remain open year-round. People, families, came from all over the world, multi-generations, aunts and uncles, cousins, young and old, they came, often taking the entire house. Staying for a month, sometimes the entire summer. Year after year they came. These were the days when those who came had only one goal in mind, and that was to rest.

Life, their lives, were hard. Just a simple task, like bathing a child, took buckets of water fetched from a well or a nearby river. Cooking a meal from food they grew on land they worked, day and night. And these were the people of some means. Before the big wars. They worked, they saved, they came to Deep Lake House. These were good people. They never caused trouble. They did what they came to do, rest.

Some people have been with me for years. They've become friends, almost family, of Deep Lake House. And generations have passed on their traditions of spending a week, a month, or the summer at the House.

But later, other people came to Deep Lake House. Different people. The kind you don't want to see coming and can't wait for them to leave. Many of them had money passed down to them, their fingers manicured and idle. Never worked a day in their lives, they came to Deep Lake House because they were bored. They wanted only a distraction, an excuse to forget how empty their lives were, how shallow their dreams. They were looking for meaning, but had no idea how or where to find it. They had parties and they were loud and had no respect for property, often throwing a bottle against my walls. All they cared about was how much fun they could have. Bed spreads were thrown on the floor and trampled. Towels brought down to the lake and lost or came back torn and sometimes covered in blood or a variety of food so pressed into the cotton that it was unrecognizable as to what created the stains. They had no concern for me and the damages they were inflicting. Their attitude always was that they could afford to pay for the damages, not realizing or caring that some items were irreplaceable and couldn't be paid for with a roll of bills.

Those were painful times.

My days may be numbered but I would be remiss if I didn't share the stories, at least a few of the ones that penetrated the walls right through to my soul, to the very core of my being, regardless of the cement or bricks or wood that lines the beams and structure of Deep Lake House. If I didn't, it would be like a human knowing they had a history unlike any ever told and keeping it to themselves, leaving those memories deep and buried.

One of my favorite guests was Miss Maisy Tuttle. She was as sweet as clover honey and as bright as the sun on new-fallen snow. The light seemed to shine down on her and follow her into whatever room she entered. She wanted only to enjoy all that the House had to offer which so many others enjoyed: the tranquility and calming rhythm of the gentle waves only a lake can provide, where you could be alone with your own thoughts without interruption, sitting for hours on the front porch, or absorbing the sun's rays down at the beach area. Always writing or reading, she brought her work with her to the House. But mostly, she gazed out at the lake that was likely as deep as her thoughts. She came for many years until she didn't. To this day I miss her brightness and calm manner.

A few years after Miss Tuttle first arrived, a young man, Mr. Mitchell Stewart came to Deep Lake House. Although most people came to rest and relax, Mr. Stewart came to work. A novelist, or a would-be one, he seemed to enjoy the quiet and solitude the House gave him. An occasional stroll or hike in the woods around the property seemed to clear his mind and would send him back to his room for hours. And then the sound of a typewriter was all that could be heard if you happened to pass by his door. He often took his meals in his room, coming out only to stretch his legs and again clear his mind for another burst of inspiration. Until he met Miss Tuttle.

The Boydins, a retired couple, had three children, who, when grown up with families of their own, visited while the Boydins were at the House, bringing their spouses and children. They loved having all of their children and grandchildren visiting but they also loved having the House to themselves, spending long hours at dinner or sitting at the beach, each with a book in hand. They chatted and laughed together, happy in their own world where only the two of them lived. They took the paddle boats out on the lake and sometimes raced back to shore, laughing the entire time, falling into each other's arms when they arrived. You never saw one without the other; they were so much in love and spent all of their time together. They just wouldn't have it any other way.

Miss Loretta Jordan was a favorite at the House because when she was here, there was always music. Everyone loved it and even those who didn't sing would hum along. Until she lost her voice. But still, she would bring her own phonograph and play her songs from her travels around the world when her voice was at its peak. You could find her sitting on the porch, tears in her eyes as she mouthed the words to the music that drifted out the window of her room. For many years the guests waited, hoping to hear the songs that brought such joy to them all, but mostly to Miss Loretta.

The Whitmores were a very traditional family, not unlike many of the families that came to Deep Lake House. Perhaps a bit wealthier than the others. The husband engaged in all the sports the area had to offer, though never bringing his wife or any of their three children to partake in these activities with him. His mother, also, was always there. At first, it seemed like she was company for the wife. But it became evident she was only there to torment the wife and control the children, and to keep all of them away from her son. A sad group, they did not bring much joy to the House. They only added to the numerous stories that were passed down.

Another family that was known to be scandalous, particularly during the 1920s when they arrived at Deep Lake House, was the Cohens. Recognized as a typical American family, they were complete with a husband, wife, and two daughters. And a nanny. When the couple first came to Deep Lake House, they were young and fun and enjoyed each other's company. Then something happened during their time away from the House and the fun was gone from their relationship.

The nanny took care of the children when the couple went out to dinner and by all outward appearances everything was fine. But the husband's long absences from his bed left many unanswered questions.

A young couple is always a welcome sight at the House. This hopefully means they will enjoy their stay so much that they will return year after year, bringing the usual additions to the family. But some young couples, even though there seems to be enough lust in the marriage, there just doesn't seem to be enough love. Joanna and Drake Morgenson were such a couple who lusted all night and then by day would often show harsh displays of pure rage and anger ignited by jealousy. But there is always hope. And sometimes there is letting go and moving on.

There are those who love to brag and carry on about their celebrity even when there is little to crow about and there you have Mr. Guy de Bourbon. A loud mouth, a blowhard, a wind bag if you will. Always seeking an audience, he was, and remains, a most memorable character. The days were long and the nights longer when Mr. Bourbon was staying at Deep Lake House. And the stories he told lived on long after he was gone. The perfect performer, the guests either loved him or found him intolerable. Either way, he was the most entertaining character we've ever seen at Deep Lake House.

There was only one and has never been another like the notorious Mr. Philip Donovan. Far from being a gentleman, he was among the lowest that has ever stayed at the House. Why he chose Deep Lake House can only be surmised, but most likely it was for the same reasons others, over the years, sought it out; for the quiet, solitude, and being located somewhat off the beaten path. And that was what Mr. Donovan was seeking, an environment where he could escape from the world and sink into anonymity, where no one knew his name.

There were so many others who came to stay at Deep Lake House. But I fear this is where the stories may end. It has been a most memorable life I've lived and my hope is that these few stories will somehow live on.

Philip Donovan

(1890s)

Chapter 2

With all the furtiveness of a cat, Philip Donovan entered the doors of Deep Lake House. Slinking his way to the desk, he tipped his hat to the desk clerk, young Jacob Ellis, and pushed a $100 bill towards him.

"I would like a room for a short stay." He spoke the fewest of words to get his message across to Jacob.

"Yes sir. Room 4 is available." Jacob reached for the key, but before he could hand it to the stranger, the man grabbed his arm.

"Upstairs." The man held onto Jacob's arm while Jacob switched room keys.

"Um, yes sir, room 7, go upstairs, to your left, last room on the left. If I could just have your name and..."

But the man had already taken the key and was heading for the staircase, a bag in each hand.

With a glance over his shoulder, Phil entered his room and immediately locked the door. After stashing both bags in the small closet, he went to the window to be sure he hadn't been followed. After checking around as much of the property as he could see, he lay on the bed, covered his face with his hat, and napped.

A couple of hours later he jolted awake upon hearing a knock at the door; faint at first, then a firmer knock and a voice calling out to him.

"Excuse me, hello sir, you need to come down to the front desk and register with us. We need your name and current address, please."

Phil wasn't having it and let them know he would not follow those rules.

"You've got my money, now leave me in peace."

After a short time, hearing footsteps walking away, Phil was able to, once again, fall asleep. But not before he checked the closet to be sure his two bags were safe and untouched.

Sometimes these places had spare keys and a maid would enter your room to clean it if they thought you weren't in it. He was tempted to drag a chair to the door so that if anyone tried to enter, he would hear them. Another couple of hours passed and Phil woke up hungry. He knew he had to make his way to the dining room to find something to eat. And they would want his name and address information. The less everyone knew about him the better. He could make up a name, that would keep suspicions down in case anyone around here was familiar with his name that was plastered on a few posters. And after this last job, his name would be a little more well-known. It was a big job and he and the three other men who robbed the train made off with quite a lot of money. Except Phil was the one who took it all. They were supposed to meet up at a location that they'd all agreed upon, but Phil had other plans and decided he would keep all the money and had headed in a different direction, one none of the others knew about. And that's how he ended up at Deep Lake House.

After making sure the money was tucked away as safely as possible, Phil walked downstairs to try to find the kitchen. No one was around, which was perfect, so he poked his head into the kitchen and asked if he could get a sandwich. There was one person in there, apparently cleaning up after lunch since it was late afternoon, before dinner got started.

"If I could get a sandwich, that would be great. Anything you've got will do."

"Yes sir, coming right up. Why don't you sit in the dining room and I'll bring your sandwich out to you as soon as it is ready."

"I would prefer to take the sandwich up to my room. If you could just wrap it up, I'll be on my way. And here's payment for it." Phil handed the man a $10 bill.

"Well, I don't take money here, you can pay at the front desk. Or they can put it on your room tab."

"I just want you to make me the God-damned sandwich and then I'll leave. Don't make this more difficult than it has to be."

"Yes, sir. I'll take care of it for you." The cook took the money and went about making a sandwich for the impatient man, anxious to get him out of his kitchen. Once the sandwich was made, the cook handed it to the stranger. He was definitely rough around the edges. The cook was sure he saw blood on the man's pants. He also poured the man a glass of water.

"Got anything stronger than water?"

"Um, sure," and he poured the man a shot of whiskey.

"Thanks." And the stranger left.

On his way up to his room, Phil did his best to slip by the front desk. Jacob was there and recognized him as the man whose name and address he needed. He took the opportunity to get this information now.

"Excuse me, sir, just a minute of your time, please. All I need is your name and an address. We like to keep in touch with our guests so, ..."

"Tom Wilson."

"Oh, ok, thanks Mr. Wilson. And an address?"

"My job keeps me on the road so I don't have a permanent address. If you don't mind, now, I would like to eat my sandwich."

"Of course, thank you, Mr. Wilson. And enjoy your lunch."

Phil quickly walked up the stairs before anyone else decided they needed more information from him.

Having eaten his sandwich, he worked on a plan for his next move. He knew he couldn't stay at this location too long. He had to keep moving because either the others in his gang would catch up with him or the Railroad police would. He was looking at a map, getting his bearings on where he was and where he would go next, when there was a knock on his door. He was sure this was someone he didn't want to see and reaching for his gun, walked towards the door.

"Who's is it?"

No answer. Not wanting to bring attention to himself by blowing a hole in whoever was at his door, he decided he would open the door, surprise whoever it was, and knock him out with the butt of his gun before whoever it was got a chance to shoot Phil. So that is exactly what he did, and it worked. He recognized the man as one of the gang. Taking some rope from one of the bags that contained a few necessary items for someone robbing a train, Phil quickly tied him up before he came to.

"Hello, Bob."

"Phil."

"What can I do for you?"

"What do you mean? You took all the money and ran off. We've all been looking for you so I'm sure you aren't surprised to see me."

"No, you're right. I've been expecting you. And here you are. Now, what should I do with you?"

"How about you give me my share of the money and then I'll leave. How does that sound?"

Phil thought that was pretty funny and laughed. Bob had to know he wasn't getting out of there alive.

"Look Bob, I can't let you go, so we can do this the hard way or the easy way. What do you think?"

"How about I start screaming?" Phil was surprised Bob said he would scream and stuffed a washcloth in his mouth. Phil was so fortunate he picked Deep Lake House since all the rooms had their own private bath. He would put the body in the tub and leave as quickly and quietly as he had arrived. Since Bob had found him, Phil was sure the Railroad Police couldn't be far behind. He packed up his bags and putting a pillow over Bob's head, shot him and left him in the tub, blood soaking through the pillow.

Phil waited a few minutes to be sure no one had heard the shot. He exited the room, locked the door, and putting the key in his pocket headed downstairs and towards the front door.

It was surprisingly quiet in the House; not a soul was around. Phil quickly walked to the front door. Opening it and stepping out into the lowering sun, Phil heard the click of a trigger and jumped back inside right as the first shots hit the front door. One shot clipped his shoulder before he got inside. He slouched down to the floor, figuring out his next move.

"We've got the place covered, Phil. Come out with your hands up."

There was no way that was going to happen. Phil knew they would gun him down. The best he could do was to go out fighting. And that was what he did. With a gun in each hand, Phil opened the door, ran out onto the porch and into the front yard with guns blazing. Within minutes he was down, his life, and the search for the stolen money, over.

Although Deep Lake House had suffered minor damages, the Railroad Police guaranteed the railroad company would pay for the damages. Within a few months, everything at Deep Lake House was back to normal. The House never suffered damage from a shoot-out again.

The Cohens

(1920s)

Chapter 3

Some guests to the House start out as the kind of guests you wish they all could be. And then something changes and you can't wait for them to leave and hope to never see them again. This was the story of the Cohens.

The year was 1922. Helen and Carl were newly married and they spent their two-week honeymoon at Deep Lake House. A fun-loving couple, young and vibrant, they hiked, they boated, and as most honeymoon couples do, they spent a good amount of time in their room, calling down for room service throughout the day. They had eyes only for each other. Their love was spread across their faces, squeezing out of the ends of their eyes, bubbling over with their smiles.

They both loved the sun, the beach, the water, and laughter surrounded them wherever they went. I looked forward to many more years of visits from the Cohens, hoping to see their children and their children's children come back to Deep Lake House year after year.

As to be expected, the next year they arrived with their first child along with additional luggage: stroller, crib, and bags of toys, bottles, and diapers. Tension began to seep into their marriage; Mrs. Cohen was too hot and uncomfortable to think about doing anything other than sitting in the cool lake water while watching her newborn. Mr. Cohen tried to recapture the magic the House seemed to exude that had bewitched the couple the previous year. But I knew it wasn't the House, it was the Cohens themselves that were special. Somehow they had forgotten what that special something was, spending more and more time alone in their all-consuming misery.

The two weeks seemed to drag on. Neither Cohen was happy. I wasn't sure if I would ever see the Cohens at Deep Lake House again. But, the next year they did arrive. Mrs. Cohen was pregnant, but appeared happy. Whatever problems they'd had the previous year now seemed to be resolved. There was love in the air around the Cohens once more. It was a loving and stress-free two weeks and the House was relieved. The little one seemed to bring only joy to the couple. I hoped their second child would be as comforting to them.

It is always surprising to me to see how much two people can change over the years. Couples once so close but now so far apart from each, it seems they're completely different people from who they once were. But couples can, similar to a house, change over the years, wear and tear showing through, as each may grow in different directions.

Although a house may seem to grow mostly older and more worn in many areas, a new owner will bring in fresh paint, new and colorful furnishings to brighten each room, and a smile for every guest who enters the house and all of this seems to seep into the very wood fibers that hold the walls together.

A couple, as they age, often become wiser even though they are more wrinkled versions of their younger selves. They are mostly happier with who they are now and are able to accept the decisions they've made in their life together, despite the path they've taken to get to where they are now.

But sometimes, just as a house only grows older as the paint fades, ceilings crumble, floors crack and split, and with structural damage setting in all hope for revival is gone, people also give up, losing track of who they are and what is most important to them. They long for the simple pleasures that once brought satisfaction, and end up destroying what is right in front of them, what they have now, as well as the lives of those closest to them.

The Cohens didn't reappear at the House for a couple of years but when they did, the two girls were now 3 and 5 years old, the bitter seed seemed to have reappeared, spreading anger like the flu through the family. So many more pieces of baggage, so many curse words exchanged between the two Cohens, so much unhappiness. Now there was a third adult privy to all the yelling and anger that the Cohens shared, and her name was Colleen. She was the nanny. A pretty young thing, small-waisted and full-bosomed, no one would ever believe that Mrs. Cohen had selected such a young beauty. Acting mother to the two girls when Mrs. Cohen was unavailable, Colleen seemed to take little interest in the children preferring instead to lay on the beach in her inappropriate bathing outfit that bared her legs, brought stares from the men, and glares from the ladies who were staying at the House.

When Mr. and Mrs. Cohen went to the dining room to eat or drove to a nearby restaurant, Colleen was the caretaker for the two girls. She mostly sat in the room, painting her nails or flipping through an issue of Life magazine, allowing the girls to run up and down the hallway, screaming and laughing, upsetting many of the other guests. The gossip whispered around the House was that Colleen was a gold-digger and a mistress to Mr. Cohen. If she was, Mrs. Cohen never said a word about it. She wasn't the kind of woman to remain silent about such a scandal so there were those at the House who didn't think it was true. Vera, the front desk manager, did her best to keep the rumors at bay by admonishing the staff not to discuss the Cohens and what went on behind their closed doors while at Deep Lake House.

The tension could be felt whenever anyone needed to talk to Mrs. Cohen, particularly the wait staff. Often showing up for breakfast or lunch alone, Mrs. Cohen at first seemed unappreciative of the service she received, but just as quickly would apologize in a manner that bordered on deep depression, often very near tears. Vera decided she needed to step in when one of the young waitresses came to her, red-faced, untying her apron, and ready to quit. Vera walked up to the table where Mrs. Cohen sat, sipping her coffee and smoking a cigarette. As Vera approached, Mrs. Cohen put out the cigarette and reaching for Vera's hand, pushed the other chair out for her to sit. Vera nearly turned to leave when she saw the dark circles and red pleading eyes laced with pain that stared up at her. But not one to run from a distressed woman, Vera sat down.

"Oh Vera, I'm so sorry I've caused the young girl trouble. I didn't mean it, really. I don't know why I'm so out of sorts these days. It's just that, well, I really don't know. Or maybe I just shouldn't say. I don't mean to burden you, or anyone, about this. This is my trouble and I need to take care of matters. But please, my apologies to the young girl. I do love Deep Lake House. It's just that, things have changed so much for me."

"Yes, I know, you have two daughters now. They can definitely change your life, children can. And don't worry, the young girl, Mary, is fine. I told her she could go home for the day. She was a bit upset."

"Again, I'm sorry to have upset her. It was misdirected anger and I should not have taken it out on her. I should not have. Please apologize for me."

"Of course. I hope your anger is not at the House, Mrs. Cohen. I hope everything has been satisfactory for you and your family."

"Please, Vera, call me Helen. And yes, very satisfactory, as always. The House is not the problem at all. Not at all. Definitely not the House. Or any of the staff either. No, no, it is much deeper than that. Much deeper." Mrs. Cohen began to contemplate her hands, rubbing them together, touching her nails, one by one as if polishing them with her finger tips.

Vera saw the sad and distressed look on Mrs. Cohen's face and reached a hand out across the table. She was well aware of the situation in this world for women and how men ruled without concern for women's wants or needs. Men were the ones who had the world in the palm of their hands while women held on to the edge by their fingertips, hoping not to fall off where they would be lost forever. Vera was very lucky in that regard; her husband, Ivan, was as good as a man could ever be. When her son started school, Vera was determined to make a living wage and since they had settled in this part of the world, with a nice plot of land that Ivan worked to feed them, Vera found Deep Lake House and fell in love, just like so many others did.

Mrs. Cohen saw Vera's extended hand and looking into Vera's eyes, so full of sympathetic concern, Mrs. Cohen couldn't stop a tear from escaping the corner of her eye. She reached out to cover Vera's warm hand and they clasped each other's hands tightly. Then Vera, always ready, took a handkerchief from her pocket and handed it to Mrs. Cohen.

"I'm so sorry to behave this way." Vera waited; Mrs. Cohen appeared ready to reveal more and Vera was there to listen.

"Sometimes life doesn't quite work out the way you expect it to. Even if you thought you had it all planned out. Even if it started out one way, exactly the way you had imagined, but then suddenly everything is changed. Nothing is how you had planned. Nothing feels right anymore. The rules change and no one has told you. You have to figure it out for yourself. And you just don't know where to go from here. You no longer know where you belong." Mrs. Cohen looked up at Vera, her eyes begging for understanding. The two women continued to hold hands. Vera felt tears coming into her own eyes. Again, she thought about her own life and how happy she was with Ivan and their son, Sven. She never knew the kind of pain and suffering that Mrs. Cohen was obviously experiencing. Vera didn't want to leave Mrs. Cohen, but she needed to get back to work. Lunchtime was ending and she needed to begin preparing the staff for dinner and check to be sure all the rooms had been cleaned. Sensing that she had taken up enough of Vera's time, Mrs. Cohen dropped the patient woman's hand and busied herself by pushing her lunch dishes away.

"I've taken up far too much of your time. I'm sure you have many other people to attend to, Vera. But I thank you for your kindness. I must get back to my girls now."

Vera was uncomfortable letting the woman leave so abruptly and reached out to touch her arm as Mrs. Cohen turned to leave the dining room.

"Are you sure you are alright now?"

Mrs. Cohen's sharp side returned and snapped her words at Vera.

"No fuss. I'm fine now. Good day." And she turned and left the room, tossing Vera's handkerchief on the table.

The next day Mr. and Mrs. Cohen were seen heading down to the beach with the girls running ahead, screaming and laughing the entire way. A motorboat, complete with cover and accommodations below deck, awaited them and they all climbed in. Carl was a fine boatsman and had his own boat at the ocean near their home. The day was spent motoring around the lake, stopping at a few spots for the girls to go in the water and swim while Helen joined them. Once a very athletic swimmer, Helen spent a lot of her time teaching her young girls to swim while wearing their life jackets. She stayed close and when she saw they were tiring, with Carl's help and the ladder at the back of the boat, they climbed back on board.

Once they were all on deck, they went below to have a bite for lunch. Helen, feeling refreshed from the short swim in the water, remembered the potential she'd once had to be a competitive diver, but had decided not to pursue once Carl had come along. He promised her the sun, the moon, and the stars and she bought it, falling head over heels in love with him. Her regrets were few, but at times like these, when she had the opportunity to swim, she thought about the life she might have had. She would never trade her girls for the world; Heidi and Ginny were the greatest gifts she had ever received. But still, what about her? What might she have done with her life, what accomplishments might she have achieved that she could be proud of besides making two babies. It now seemed that her only goal in life was to see her girls grow and flourish. Was that enough? Her dreams, once so full and open to possibilities, now felt stale and tarnished, much like her marriage was turning.

They finished lunch, mostly in silence, the girls giggling while they ate, and then it was time to head back to the House. Again, the silence, sometimes so deafening, escorted them back to the beach and dock area. The girls were ready for naps as was Helen. Carl would do what he always did, something for his amusement alone. As the days went by Helen had her suspicions what his amusements might be and with whom he did them. But she was used to keeping her mouth shut, keeping it bottled up until it exploded out of her like it had at breakfast the day before. She felt like she no longer had control of her emotions.

Back in their rooms, the girls settled in for naps, and after taking a quick sponge bath, Helen was ready to go down to dinner. She called down for a couple of sandwiches for the girls that would be brought up by Colleen after the girls finished napping. Carl had also changed and was ready to go. Dinner was quick and satisfying, but Helen felt the day's activities catching up with her and knew she was in for an early night.

"So, care for a night cap?" Carl was fond of an after-dinner glass of brandy or scotch. He was also fond of the bar at the House and enjoyed meeting the other guests.

"Oh, none for me. I can barely keep my eyes open. So, I'll see you in the morning." Carl gave her his usual peck on the cheek and Helen left to go back to their room. She hoped Colleen had taken care of feeding the girls and when she checked on them, they were both fast asleep. Back in her room, she washed her face and changed into her nightgown, crawled under the covers and fell fast asleep.

Something woke Helen and her first thought was the girls. She quickly went next door but found them both still breathing deeply. When she came back to her room, she checked the clock on the nightstand and noticed that it was 1:52am. Carl was not in his bed. She knew where he was. She always knew where he was when he disappeared in the middle of the night. Suddenly something went off in her head like a little explosion, similar to how she felt when her rudeness took over and Vera had to step in to remind her to act in a more civil manner in the dining room. But now she was in her room and now there was only one person to take this anger, this frustration, this sad situation that was now her life out on. Putting on her bathrobe and grabbing the room key, she quickly went down the hall and down the staircase to the room where Colleen was staying. She approached quietly and stood listening at the door. The thick walls and heavy doors provided a lot of privacy, but Helen could still hear talking, giggling, moaning and what she imagined was kissing. She knocked on the door. The room went silent. Then she knocked a little louder.

"I know you're in there, Carl. Come out right now. Leave your whore and come back upstairs with your wife."

People started opening doors, peeking out to see who was making a ruckus. Helen stared back at them, and let them know, let everyone know, what was going on in the room where she stood.

"It's my husband and our nanny, who is also my husband's whore. What do you think of that? Isn't that a wonderful surprise at 2am? Your husband fucking the whore who cares for your children. Although how much care she actually gives them, when she isn't polishing her nails or reading her magazine, would be a surprise to me. Did you remember to feed them tonight, Colleen? Or were you too busy fucking my husband?" The guests all quickly went back into their rooms and Helen, also, went back to her room. The explosion that went off inside her was now gushing out of her like a waterfall and she couldn't get back to her room quickly enough before the tears blurred her way. Once inside, she grabbed a pillow and screamed out the poison that had invaded her lungs, her stomach, her heart.

Exhausted, Helen soon fell asleep. She was woken by knocking at the door and heard her girls calling out to her. She jumped from bed and rushed to greet them.

"Oh, my sweet girls. I'm so sorry you woke alone. Let mom get dressed and I'll bring you to breakfast, ok?" They had both tried to dress themselves but needed a little help, so first Helen took care of her girls and then quickly put on her own clothes. Helen noticed that Carl's bed had not been slept in, which did not surprise her at all. Together they walked down to the dining room.

At the dining room, Helen looked around but there was no sign of Carl. She was sure he was still sleeping with his whore. The girls each had oatmeal and Helen just had coffee. Although she was a ball of knots inside, she did her best to appear calm for her daughters. Her thoughts, of course, were focused on

Carl and Colleen and what her next step should be. She knew she had to face Carl – he would be livid with Helen's performance outside Colleen's room at 2am. But Helen didn't care. She would leave him. He would support her and her children and she would get a job. She used to be a secretary, once she gave up her dream of being a competitive diver and when she and Carl first married, before he started making money. She could do that again. She enjoyed working in an office. She didn't care, she would do whatever she needed to do. She would never again be a wife who knows her husband has a mistress but looks the other way. She thought she and Carl were stronger than that, she thought their love was real. But she knew the truth now; she was the nanny and Colleen was his wife. And that simply would not work for her.

Suddenly, her arm was grabbed and she was being lifted from her chair. It was Carl, who quickly directed her to the front door, apparently not wanting to cause a scene in the dining room. Helen looked back at the girls and saw Colleen sitting down next to them.

Outside, Carl, still directing Helen by her arm, moved her to their Packard and helping her get inside, locked the door and got into his side. He drove off the property and down the road to a clearing and pulling in, got out of the car.

"What is wrong with you, woman? Have you gone mad?"

"Carl, you can't be serious! I know you were in there with Colleen, I know she is now your whore." Carl reached out and slapped Helen across the face. She put her hand to her face and fought back the tears, and instead felt only shock. Never had Carl ever hit her. And at that moment, she knew he never would again.

He reached out, shocked at his own behavior. "Helen, I'm sorry, I didn't mean…"

"You didn't mean what, to hit your wife while defending the woman you hired as our nanny and who has become your whore? Is that what you didn't mean to do? What I do know, Carl, is that you will never hit me, you will never touch me, again. I want a divorce!"

Divorce, to Carl, meant failure. He was successful at his company and the boss wanted happily-married men. Carl might even lose his job if his boss thought his wife wanted a divorce.

"Look, I said I'm sorry. Let's work this out, shall we? I'll fire Colleen, we can get another nanny. Or maybe you just need to get to know her a little better, she really is a sweet person."

"Ha! Sweet to you, I'm sure. No thanks, I don't want her near my children. Take me back to the House now, Carl."

"I don't want a divorce Helen and I won't give you one."

"It doesn't matter, Carl, I'm leaving you. That's all there is to it." Helen got back in the car and waited for Carl to take her back to the House. Carl paced, trying to think of what he could say to convince Helen to stay with him. He didn't want to fire Colleen; he was in love with her. Maybe he could find another way. He got in the car and drove back to the House.

Helen quickly packed all their belongings. They were ending their vacation only two days early, they could make an excuse that Carl had to get back for work. Before leaving, Helen made sure she gave Vera her address and told her she would be in touch.

The next year, Carl arrived again, reserving the same two weeks as he and Helen always had. But this time, Helen was not with him. Instead, a pregnant Colleen accompanied him. She was the same self-centered, simple-minded ingenue she was when she was Carl and Helen's nanny. She complained endlessly and if Carl didn't take care of her needs immediately, she voiced her unhappiness. He knew that Deep Lake House was not a place where unsophisticated young ladies frequented. Carl took care of the business of checking them in, his frustration obvious when Vera greeted him.

"Hello Mr. Cohen. Just you and the nanny, is it Colleen, this time?"

"Actually, she is my wife now, Vera."

"Oh, how is Mrs. Cohen, I'm sorry, I mean, Helen? I hope she is fine."

"No, I'm sorry to say, the former Mrs. Cohen had an accident. She was prone to experiencing dizzy spells and was sleep-walking and fell down the stairs, I'm afraid, breaking her neck. This happened not long after we returned home last year. It has been about 10 months now. Very tragic, it was, for the girls."

Vera, who had just received a letter the day before from Helen Cohen, who had returned to her maiden name of Helen Carmichael, suppressed a smile, feigning genuine sympathy for Carl who was trying his best to convince Vera his grief was real.

At that moment, Colleen, the new Mrs. Cohen, stood at the entrance to Deep Lake House.

"Carl, if you are done chit-chatting with the lady, do you think you can bring our bags in so I can take a nap. I'm exhausted and I need to rest. Also, I need some food, I'm starved so bring me a sandwich if it's not too much trouble."

Carl, sighing deeply, shook his head as Vera handed him the key to their room.

"Enjoy your stay, Mr. Cohen."

Guy de Bourbon

(1930s)

Chapter 4

The front door burst open like with the winds of a tornado whose goal was to rip the roof off the House, at the very least. Immediately the voice, the accent indecipherable but trying its best to imitate a Frenchman, was sonorous and slightly musical in its desire to grab everyone's attention. And without fail, it did. All eyes were on him; he was in his element, basking in the glow of his own self-importance.

"Good day, mes amis. Bonjour, bonjour! Monsieur Guy de Bourbon has arrived." The man was tall, slim, attired in a white shirt with full front ruffles, covered by a burgundy velvet vest and matching tailcoat with black fitted pants, topped off with a top hat, wearing short boots and carrying short black gloves. A vision like nothing anyone had ever seen at Deep Lake House, he was quite pleased with the reactions he beheld at his entrance.

There is always one person, typically a man, who does his best to get the attention of everyone within earshot of his voice. In the House, there is the dining area and also the living room area where people can sit in cozy groups and read or chat. Usually quietly. But when someone invades that quiet space with a booming voice that demands everyone's attention, it can be quite disrupting to an individual's focus, particularly if their intention is to read. This was how Guy de Bourbon presented himself. From the moment he entered the doors of Deep Lake House, Mr. Bourbon caused a scene straight out of the motion pictures; drama, intrigue, and everyone's undivided attention were what he craved above all else. Hoping, always, to make himself the subject of all conversations.

Vera Swansons, desk clerk for several years now at the House, thought she had seen it all at Deep Lake House but never had she seen anyone like Mr. Bourbon. A term like "fancy pants" came to mind, or even a buffoon, although the other guests did seem to be intrigued by the new guest. While he stood and basked in all the attention, Vera waited for Mr.

Bourbon to turn to her. After a few minutes when the other guests had turned back to their own business, Mr. Bourbon finally gave his attention to Vera.

"Welcome, Mr. Bourbon."

"Monsieur."

"Excuse me?"

"I am Monsieur de Bourbon, s'il vous plaît."

"Oh, ok. Monsieur de Bourbon. Just fill out the information on this form, please. And your room is on the first floor, #3, down the hall here and to your right." Mr. Bourbon pulled out a wad of francs to pay for the room.

"We do not take French currency here, Mr...Monsieur de Bourbon. You'll have to pay in American dollars."

"Mais oui, of course, pardonnez-moi." Monsieur de Bourbon took a small purse from his tailcoat and handed a few dollars to Vera.

"How long will you be staying, Monsieur de Bourbon?"

"Un peu de temps, a week or two, perhaps."

"Then you can pay for your room at that time, since you are unsure of how long you will be staying. Just let us know a day or two before you plan on leaving."

"Tres bien." And Mr. Bourbon headed to his room, glancing at the patrons to see if he still had their attention. He did.

In his room, Guy stood in front of the window, looking out at the comings and goings of several of the guests at the House. While he waited for the bell boy to bring his trunk to the room, he planned his daily activities. He shone brightest at night – he had always been attracted to the bright lights of the stage. Although not a film actor himself, he knew he could play any role that he auditioned for and often thought about leaving the stage and going to Hollywood. This week would be his greatest performance. Although he would barely be performing since he billed himself as a descendant of King Louis XVIII and his anticipation at watching the guests' reaction to this news was more than he could bear. A showman always first, the attention was what he craved.

Having grown up in Oradell, New Jersey, and named after his grandfather, Guy Blauvelt, Guy had always been a performer. Whenever there was an event in town with actors performing on a stage, Guy was there and would come home to imitate what he had seen, receiving much applause from the family. With four older brothers and sisters, he never lacked an audience. Since he was the youngest, he was given more attention than all the others put together, spoiled by all of them, which started him on his way to craving attention. He knew at the young age of seven that the stage was for him.

He left home at the age of 17 and traveled to New York to seek his fame and fortune as an actor. He had participated in the plays at school and knew he had learned as much as he could. He heard about New York through the magazines his sisters got, like Life Magazine. So, with a few dollars in his pocket, he traveled by train to New York. By this time, his older brothers and sisters were all married. Fortunately, they lived close to their parents so Guy knew they would be taken care of without him at home. His family would all miss him, but they were all very excited to have an actor in the family. None of the Blauvelt's had ever left Oradell before, so this was a huge event in the family.

The train took Guy to New York City where he searched for the cheapest boarding house he could find. During the day he scoured the city, looking for free events where actors performed, learning their trade. In the evenings, he'd perform before the small mirror above the sink in the bathroom that he shared with the other boarders. It wasn't an ideal situation but it was all Guy could afford. He found a job at night as a dishwasher in a local restaurant so he had the days to pursue his craft. Except for the hard work at the restaurant, this was a perfect situation for Guy.

An upscale restaurant, Guy would often spy on the customers, imagining he was sitting in their seats instead of watching them from the kitchen. There was one particular customer who stood out for him from among all the others. A Frenchman, with a flair unlike anything Guy had ever seen before, caused quite a flurry in the restaurant whenever he dined. He was very particular regarding his food and wouldn't hesitate if the soup was not to his liking, returning it to the kitchen. If there was a bit of pink in his duck, he would send the entire bird back. The restaurant often gave him his meal for free since the man seemed to have a lot of influence and attracted those with money to the restaurant. Guy was sure the reason was because he was so flamboyant and demanded attention.

"Garcon, where is my Cognac? I've been sitting here for more than 5 minutes now and I have not yet had a single waiter come to serve me!" Which, of course, Guy knew was not true since many servers had already brought him the menu, water, and rolls with butter.

His dress, also, was outrageous but Guy could not take his eyes off the rich-looking brocade, the satin jodhpurs, the gold buttons, and the spats that partially covered his black leather boots.

Guy tried to hear every word that was spoken and after seeing the man several times at the restaurant, one story stuck out from all the others and that was the man's connection to King Louis XVIII. He made it clear to all who cared to listen, and that was usually the entire restaurant, that he was a descendent of King Louis.

"Young man," he would address the waiter closest to him, whether or not the waiter was serving him at the time. "Did you know that my great, great, great uncle was King Louis XVIII? Oh yes, a great man he was indeed. I've been told I'm very much like him. I have greatness in me, as well. I'm Monsieur Frederick de Bourbon of the de Bourbon family from the south of France. Where is my soup? My soup should have arrived by now. If it is cold, I shall send it back to the kitchen and had better not be charged for it!"

Guy was mesmerized. The French accent was one he knew he could imitate perfectly with practice. And now he had a new mission. He needed to have a new persona and decided this was it. After all, his name was Guy, which he was told was French – there was French in their family after all. How much of a leap was it for Guy to take on the mannerisms of Monsieur de Bourbon? After all, who knows of him except those who live right in New York City. Guy would travel around the country performing and no one will know anything about Monsieur Frederick de Bourbon. Monsieur Guy de Bourbon will be famous!

Guy knew he had some research to do and so went to the library to research France and King Louis XVIII. He was also practicing the accent so that he would sound authentic. He wanted to be a showman and this was his big chance. He was very excited about his new persona and decided he needed to start getting into character.

Over the years, this all worked out for Guy – he got stage parts when a production needed a French man. He never let it slip that he was from New Jersey. His character became so effortless, that the line between Guy Blauvelt and Guy de Bourbon was nearly imperceptible. He liked this person; he was so confident and so much more interesting than Guy Blauvelt had ever been. And he loved the attention. Just like he used to get when he was a boy. This is what he was always trying to recreate; the experience where he entertained to astounding applause.

And now at Deep Lake House, Guy was preparing himself for an evening of showmanship. He was always looking for occasions to entertain and he had gotten many jobs this way. He was sure Deep Lake House would be a golden opportunity for him.

He prepared himself for dinner, dressing up in his most lavish outfit, and made his way down to the dining room. As only a few persons were seated, Guy considered going back to his room and waiting until the dining room would perhaps have more patrons. But he might come back and no seats would be available, so he decided to spend his time sipping a cocktail before ordering dinner. Surely others would show up in that time and he would be more relaxed and ready for the crowd.

Whereas Monsieur Frederick de Bourbon of New York only sat in his chair, ate his meal, and entertained the crowds simply by being himself, Monsieur Guy de Bourbon of New Jersey would interact directly with the patrons in the dining room so that they would more intimately know all about Guy de Bourbon, whether they cared to or not. Guy had received such high praise for his character that he was sure he would thrill the crowds no matter where he performed.

After being seated, Guy was served Cognac, the only drink he ever heard Monsieur Frederick de Bourbon order and so it had become his drink as well. He sipped while watching the dining room slowly fill up. And then he ordered his meal; always a modest fare, watching his wallet, a bowl of soup and a boule with herbed soft butter would suffice. While enjoying the scant dinner, Guy waited for the perfect opportunity to engage with his audience. He had thought of checking with Vera, the woman at the front desk, but thought better of it since she very well may have said 'no', that she didn't want the guests bothered while enjoying their meals. Instead, he decided to just go from table to table to feel out the crowd to see if they would be receptive to a show of sorts.

Once he had finished his soup and very nearly all of his bread, he stood to make his way from table to table, introducing himself as a descendent of King Louis XVIII. The crowd was as he had hoped; quite entertained and amused at the attire and flourish of his extravagant gestures as he shook the men's hands and kissed the hands of the ladies. The men smiled and laughed, the ladies blushed and fanned themselves having never even met a French man much less be kissed by one. Although not an overly handsome man, the outfit and his charming manners made him more attractive than he would have been if he had been wearing street clothes.

His banter with the crowd and their enjoyment of Monsieur Guy de Bourbon, kept the entire dining room mesmerized. The waiters worked their way around Monsieur Guy and smiled at him, appreciating how he kept the guests so well occupied that no one dared to interrupt to ask for another drink, waiting until the show was over. The waiters were then able to serve the meals without interruption, making their jobs easier.

When Monsieur Guy de Bourbon got to his regular routine where he talked about his great, great, great uncle, King Louis XVIII, the crowd was more than impressed, many of the women even applauding. And then it happened, something Guy never expected would ever happen and brought him to a standstill while he caught his breath. A woman's voice called out, barely loud enough for all to hear, which meant she was close by but Guy could not tell at which table she sat.

"So, you must be related to Monsieur Frederick de Bourbon, oui?" Her accent was perfect French, even better than Guy's. Was she a relative of Monsieur Frederick or an entertainer like Guy himself? Guy had to find her without giving away his secret.

"But of course." And then he quickly moved onto the next table, back to his charming ways. While making his way back to his own table, he stood in the middle of the room and, bowing low, thanked them all for their time.

"I wish you all a delicious meal and a charming stay at Deep Lake House. Good night." And he walked out of the room to abundant applause.

He quickly made his way to his room where he locked the door and sat on his bed, wondering what to do about this person who could possibly destroy his act. He had to find her. But how?

He thought he would go incognito and search the House, hoping to find her out before she could do any damage to his reputation. He decided to change into plain clothes so that no one would recognize him, when there was a knock at the door. He jumped and sat back down on his bed, deciding whether or not to answer.

"Monsieur de Bourbon? Guy de Bourbon? Are you in there?" He was sure it was the same woman from the dining room.

"Yes, it is I, I am in here, yes. What is it you want?" He felt confused and unsure if he should even answer the door. He didn't know if he really wanted to find out about this woman. Would he know her, could he possibly have met her at one of the shows where he had performed? Was she also a performer? Or was she there to let everyone know he was a fraud and that he stole his character from a real man and maybe she was related to Monsieur Frederick de Bourbon of New York? He was considering these possibilities when, again, another knock came from the door.

"Monsieur? I want you to know, I'm a friend. I know you. You are Guy Blauvelt, correct? From New Jersey?"

Who is this person? How do they know him and that his name is Guy Blauvelt and that he is from New Jersey? Now, more curious than ever, he had to open the door to meet this woman, no longer concerned that she could ruin his reputation or expose him as a fraud.

Guy pulled open the door and there stood a small, petite, attractive woman with deep russet hair, flowing past her shoulders. She was dressed plainly but stylishly. Guy looked her up and down and stood more erect, his 6-foot frame towering over the young woman. He felt himself blush as she smiled sweetly, hiding her pleasure upon seeing the man standing in front of her.

"Guy, it is so good to see you again. I was sure it had to be you. I followed you to New York to see what you would make of yourself, you were such a talented man, and then I came here perchance, on a holiday with my great aunt. I must apologize for the comment about Monsieur Frederick de Bourbon, but I knew I wouldn't get your attention otherwise."

"So, you wish to expose me as a fraud?" Guy remained standing tall in front of the woman, not inviting her into his room but waiting to find out her motive for possibly exposing him.

"Oh, good heavens, no! Not at all! I just wanted you to know that someone in the audience knew who you really were. I was hoping it would be a great surprise. Sorry, but I seem to have failed there." The young woman hung her head, seemingly embarrassed by her choice of a charade.

"But who are you? How do you know me?" Guy was still not sure he even knew this young woman and thought perhaps she was just a forlorn fan, longing to meet a bright and upcoming star such as himself.

"So, you do not remember me? Well, then it is not such a great surprise for you. I'm truly sorry to have bothered you, Guy." And the young woman began to back away from the door.

"No, please, I've been to so many cities and performed so many places, I can't possibly remember all the admirers I've met in my life. Please, come in and sit." He offered the young woman a chair by the door while he sat on the edge of his bed.

"Would you like something to drink? Oh, I'm sorry, I really do not have anything to offer you but we could go down to the dining room, although it is probably still full with guests eating their dinner." He waited for the woman to speak again, to hopefully explain who she was and how she knew so much about Guy, the real Guy.

After much hesitation, as if composing her thoughts, the woman finally did speak.

"First, I will start by telling you my name. It is Marie Saunders. And I grew up in Oradell, New Jersey." She stopped here to let this information sink in, hoping it would spark some memory in Guy. But still nothing.

"So, did I know you in Oradell?" He still seemed confused.

"Oh, yes, you did Guy. We were friends in our younger years. And then you left when you were just a teen, to pursue fame and fortune. I always admired you so much for taking that brave step forward, to live your dream." Her eyes glowed with the admiration Guy had seen in the eyes of so many fans over the years. But this was different.

"Thank you, Marie. That is very kind of you."

"But still, Guy, no recognition?" Guy thought back to his time in Oradell and the many people he knew. He was so interested in the performing that he never really paid much attention to others around him. But there was this one girl who had captured his heart in his first year in high school. He had been so unsure of his looks, he thought his only way to get any attention was through his performances. And that became his focus. So, he never pursued any romantic connection with her and then, after graduating, he had left for New York.

"Marie, yes, I do remember you. My apologies for it taking me so long. As I said, I've met so many young women… ah, people… over the years, and I've played Guy de Bourbon for so long, I simply forgot my roots and where I came from. But now it has all come back to me. Yes, yes, I do remember you, very much."

Marie's face lit up and her smile grew so wide that Guy saw the young woman he knew from Oradell, New Jersey. And then, the awkward, insecure boy came out in Guy and he blushed at his own discomfort.

"But how did you know about Monsieur Frederick de Bourbon?"

"Well, as I told you, I am here with my aunt, who I must get back to. She likes to walk on the porch after dinner. I have become her traveling companion and she does enjoy traveling. We had been to New York several times and I saw you at the New Yorker Hotel where you worked in the kitchen, is that not correct?"

"It is true. I was there for a couple of years and watched Monsieur Frederick every chance I got, perfecting the character I was destined to play. And his character has been successful, people seem to enjoy his outrageous clothes and his pompous attitude." Guy had to laugh, realizing how unlike Monsieur Frederick de Bourbon was from Guy Blauvelt.

The two sat and looked at each other, glowing in their shared memories. Guy had no one like this in his life since he traveled from town to town. His parents had passed on and his siblings were all busy in their lives with their children. A couple of times his sisters had come to see his shows and they shared a dinner, laughing like in the old days, both so proud of Guy. His brothers he saw less often, but he did send them post cards from places where he was performing. His sisters assured him they loved the post cards, they were both so busy with their jobs and their families and sent Guy their love. And now he wanted to spend more time with Marie and get to know the grown-up woman she had become.

"How long are you and your aunt staying at Deep Lake House?"

"We are here just for the week. And then we are going back to New Jersey for a short time before our travels resume. If you do not have any more performances, why don't you come with us? I'm sure your family would love to see you again." Although it sounded like a great idea, Guy knew he had to work, although he had managed to save a bit of his money. But taking any time off caused him anxiety – he was sure his admirers would forget him. And he needed to continue to grow his popularity and find more jobs. He had a few jobs lined up in different locations on the east coast and hoped to set up a schedule here at Deep Lake House. But a short vacation might be possible. And to renew a friendship, or rather to begin a friendship, with the lovely Marie might be exactly what he needed.

"I believe I will join you. I would love to see my family again, it has been years, even though my sisters have attended a couple of my performances. But you know mostly, Marie, I would love to get to know more about you. I do remember I had quite a crush on you back in school but thought you did not care for me. I was too shy, which is why I loved to perform. I could be someone else."

"Oh Guy, I thought you were so interesting. I was so hoping you would ask me for a date but you never did. I thought you weren't interested in me." Guy knelt down in front of Marie and looking into her sparkling bright blue eyes, took her hands in his, and kissed them softly. He was sure that out of all of his performances, none could compare to the one now taking place. For this performance was the most honest Guy had ever felt. This one came from his heart and a growing love he felt blooming inside his chest.

The Whitmores

(1940s)

Chapter 5

There are some families that come to stay at the House who bring with them a feeling of dread and premonition of unfortunate things to come. That was the feeling that permeated my front entrance, the walls, the floors, wherever the Whitmores walked.

The children, two boys 8 and 10, and a girl 6, were oblivious to the tension the adults carried inside them. Or so it seemed since the acting out and high-levels of activity were more than a little excessive, even for children their ages. The father, a man living in his own world of sport-related activities, appeared as oblivious to the tension as the children, perhaps even more so.

But the wife and the mother-in-law, completely at odds on all topics, here was the source of all the tension that blanketed every member of the Whitmore family. Never a word was spoken by the wife where a criticism, a chastisement as if to scold a child for laughing too loudly while playing on the swings, came like a slap from the mother-in-law. Every time.

All I could do, as I always do, was to watch and weep for a doomed family, an unhappy wife, a woman stuck in a familiar situation common to so many women during the 1940s. Wanting more from life than the role of a mother to her spoiled children and a wife to a delinquent husband whose concerns are only those that he deems worthy of his time and that do not include his wife or children. The sadness hung over her like a razon-edged pendulum, wondering when it would reach its host. Not getting the support and attention she so craved from her husband, the wife knew her place and it was always behind the only person who her husband listened to, the one who ruled his house, his mother.

They occupied two rooms; one for the husband and wife, and one for the children and their grandmother; the boys sharing one bed, the girl sleeping with her grandmother. The mother had little contact with her children and when she did the mother-in-law would contradict or overrule whatever guidelines she tried to impress upon her children, while belittling their mother in front them. She tried in vain many times to address this uneven distribution of power in her own home, but it was a lost cause speaking to a carefree and self-centered husband who was more like another one of the children than the man of the house.

A two-week stay each year for several years turned into a time of tension for Deep Lake House, touching every vacationer unfortunate enough to be spending a week, two, or more at the same time as the Whitmores. The grandmother always yelling, the children screaming and acting out the anger their mother was so obviously trying to keep inside but one could read clearly as if it was written in black ink across her face. The saying 'children should be seen and not heard' did not apply to the Whitmore children, but rather to their mother. And if the grandmother had her way, their mother would disappear completely, never to be seen again either. I never know the reasons behind the tragic stories that come to the House, I only know what I see and hear. And this was, indeed, a tragic family, with their own sad tale.

Once settled in their rooms, the Whitmores spent a good part of their days out and about, around Deep Lake and, for the children, finding amusement in the woods around or on the property. A few times they were all seen heading out on their boat with the husband at the helm, in his element, so preoccupied that no one was allowed to bother him, whatever catastrophe befell them, short of an attack by an unforeseen force. The mother-in-law gave all of her attention to the children, directing and disciplining when she felt it was needed. Which left the wife to her own thoughts, as morbid as they so often were. Once or twice, she was told her services were needed, for example, when the mother-in-law decided it was time for lunch. Then the husband would pull off into a cove and the wife would set out the plates and silverware for each and dish up the food that the dining room at Deep Lake House had prepared for them to bring on their boat ride. She was often reduced to nothing more than a housekeeper for the family, having little interaction with her family other than to clean up after them. Although she believed her children should help out with chores, cleaning their own rooms and picking up after themselves, the mother-in-law wouldn't hear of it.

"This is play time for the children, they should not have to clean! That is their mother's job. You are their mother – do your job!"

Whenever the mother-in-law said these words, it was easy for the wife to understand how her husband came to be the self-centered individual he was, thinking only of himself and his own amusement. He never really grew up and his mother saw to it that he remained completely dependent on her for nearly all of his needs.

But the wife, Eva, was different. She wanted to see her children grow up as healthy, self-reliant individuals. She had her own aspirations that she'd had put aside when Samuel had asked her to marry him. When they took these private boat rides, or walks, or drives in the car when they were home, she would reminisce in her own mind how nice it had been when they'd first met, how much they'd enjoyed each other's company, how Samuel had pursued her and swept her off her feet with his charm and intelligence that impressed her so, and his attention to everything that was happening in Eva's life, too. He seemed to enjoy that she was a book editor who loved her job. But when they married, she left her job because soon after, she'd become pregnant. It was at that point that Samuel flew his mother in from Germany to help with Eva's pregnancy.

And now, more than ten years later, his mother was still here. And in charge. And everything between Eva and Samuel changed, drastically. She wondered if it could ever be as it once was. Maybe when the children no longer needed the old woman's help. With her youngest at 6 years old, Eva thought that maybe in less than ten years they'd be free of the old woman, finally. Or maybe she would die before that. These thoughts would enter Eva's mind in a variety of ways, when thinking about how her life was before the old woman arrived, when thinking about her future with Samuel and how much she missed what they once had, and sometimes it would just force its way in, evil in its intent, with Eva surprised at her own violent musings. She would shake these ideas from her head, fearing that others, outside of herself, somehow knew the content of her frightful brooding.

But many of her thoughts gave her pleasure and she would escape into the world where only she and Samuel lived. A world that was full of love. She would wonder what happened to that love. How could Samuel change so much and become a man she was growing to detest, a man so attached to his mother that he ignored his wife completely?

She also took great pleasure in reliving her life as a book editor. Eva was even working on her own novel, written in her mind, not on paper for fear the mother-in-law would find it, criticize and insult her, and then destroy it. She couldn't take that chance. But this is where her thoughts went while they walked in the woods, or she sat at the back of the boat, lost in her own creative mind, or in the front seat of their car on their Sunday drives through the countryside, which was the most time Eva spent with Samuel in any week. Their bedrooms at home, although attached rooms, were feeling more to Eva like a prison to her for Samuel visited her less and less frequently. Since he informed her that three children were enough, he felt no need for his wife's company. Eva struggled with this since she longed for his touch, not even sexually but just a caress, the feel of his strong arms around her, holding her, comforting her when she was feeling so alone. But it had been months, maybe even years, time had no meaning anymore, since he visited her bed. She forced a smile whenever he looked her way, but deep down her feelings for him had changed. He was no longer the man she wanted to spend her life with but had become the man she needed to escape from. He certainly was never physically abusive to her but abuse comes in so many forms. No longer feeling loved, cared for, touched, or even having her presence acknowledged by the man she'd once had such strong feelings of love for, seemed as abusive to her as if he were physically beating her. At these times she would scream her silent screams of sadness, frustration, and longing that she continued to push down deep into her soul. And smile her empty smile, devoid of feelings, reflecting only the death that lived inside of her.

And then she met Loretta. A chance meeting, Eva certainly wasn't looking for company, having spent so much of her life alone in her own thoughts. But this woman was persistent, Eva felt the woman's eyes on her, watching her movements, or since Eva was well-trained in sitting motionless for hours on end, her non-movements. And then suddenly, she recognized the woman. It was Miss Loretta Jordan, the well-known singer who years before Eva had seen in concert. After several minutes, Miss Loretta motioned to the still and silent woman to join her. Eva got up and walked to her table.

It was a brief visit, as all of Eva's alone time was, since her watchdog was never far away. And for those few precious moments, talking with Miss Loretta, Eva felt alive. But she knew it was only because for that short time she had left her reality and joined Miss Loretta as a friend and they were sharing stories about their lives, their hopes, and their dreams. It felt so real, so possible, to Eva. Until it wasn't.

The voice she knew so well, the one that haunted all her dreams and turned every loving moment into a nightmare, screamed her name, causing everyone who was in the room or nearby to look first at the screaming woman and then at Eva, who was cringing, visibly shaking with fear, anger, or frustration. You weren't sure which emotion Eva was feeling or if it was a combination of all of them. Only Eva knew what she was feeling; a loathing, a deep and menacing darkness that caused her stomach to turn on itself and urged her to run out of Deep Lake House, out of this life forever, for she feared what she might do if she stayed.

The old woman then did what she always did, she insulted Miss Loretta. Miss Loretta took the insult with grace and called for assistance from the waiter. Embarrassed beyond imagining, Eva ran outdoors and away from the old woman, who could not keep up with the much younger Eva.

Finding a rowboat, Eva jumped in and rowed until she was exhausted. The lake gave her the freedom she was looking for and she sat in the bottom of the small boat, her heart breaking as she cried out all of the life left in her. And as quietly as she had lived, she slipped into the dark waters below.

Miss Loretta

(1940s)

Chapter 6

The day Miss Loretta walked through the front door of Deep Lake House, you only had to look into her eyes to see the broken heart that beat beneath her blouse. Eyes full of tears held back by sheer force of will, she made her way to the front desk as if in a trance, wondering why she was there at all or even how she got here.

The people who I have loved the most over the many years are the ones who come to Deep Lake House for comfort, looking for a way to ease their pain. And they are hoping, sometimes it is their last hope, to find it here. I want only for them to feel the love that seeps from my joints and cracks in my walls, to know that they are finally in a place of love, as if held in a never-ending embrace, safe, finally. The heart at the core of my being broke when Loretta walked in, for I knew this was a soul who needed tender care for such a fragile spirit as hers. These were the times when I envied those who could give physical comfort in the form of a hug, assuring protection and understanding for the broken pieces that made up the whole being that often seemed to be held together with nothing more than transparent tape.

She made her way up to her room, and there she stayed, hidden away from everything and everyone who might distract her from the misery she was so attached to and unable to let go of, unable to see any light that might guide her out of the depths of depression that had swallowed her up. This was where she would find solace. This was where she would hopefully find the way to mend her broken heart and spirit. Once again.

Loretta was never bothered by the bright lights. If anyone asked, she would tell them that the lights brought out the star that had settled deep into her lungs and shone throughout her body and came out with the most magical sound, her voice. And then the crowd, rising to a crescendo with their deafening applause. A sound like a tribute, a dedication to and written only for her.

There was a time when Miss Loretta never thought she would make it to the stage, never be able to perform, never receive the praise and acclaim she so desired. When she was a child, her papa never failed to remind the girl that she would amount to nothing. He also never failed to remind her that she, and she alone, was responsible for her mama's death. Her brother, Alonzo, could do no wrong. Mama was fine and healthy after birthing him. But two years later and with the birth of the baby Loretta, just like that, without warning, mama died. The doctors said it was giving birth, it was a difficult one, they said. Papa would have nothing to do with her so her mama's mama came to care for her or she may have just faded away to dust. Curl up in her crib, go to sleep, and never wake. And papa would be fine with that. But gran'mama wouldn't have it. She did everything she could to keep that little heart pumping. She said she saw the light that shone in the baby's face and that came out of her mouth whenever she let out a coo or a cry. She would be a star, a bright shining star. And she told little Loretta that she believed in her. She told her that her mama lived on in Loretta and would be with her forever inside her.

But her papa did what he could to kill whatever dreams Loretta may have. Whenever she sang around the house, her papa would tell her to take her screeching voice outside – he didn't want to hear it. It sounded like two cats fighting. He couldn't find any room in his heart for his young daughter. He only had hate; she only brought him pain. Loretta was sure that if she didn't have gran'mama, she would have killed herself long ago. And so, she grew and flourished, the light shining bright in the small girl. She believed her gran'mama and followed the star that led her to the chorus in school, the choir at church, the stage in high school and beyond. She sang in concert halls, in dinner and night clubs, at every venue that would have her. Her voice saved her, her voice fed and clothed her, her voice gave her a good living. She had fans around the world. Wherever she went she was loved and adored by all.

And then she came to Deep Lake House. She came here because the light that had shone so brightly inside her for so long, just went out. Without notice, without reason, without any kind of a warning. She was on stage at Symphony Hall when the bright lights seemed to blind her, allowing her to see only the people in the audience, waiting for the sweet Loretta voice to entertain and move them to tears. But it never came out. A cough, a hiccup, a gasp was all that was heard. And then Loretta running off the stage and out the back door to her limo that was waiting to take her to her suite at the Park Plaza Hotel.

She was humiliated and had no idea what was happening to her. Her agent found her in her room, under the covers, crying her eyes out until there were no tears left to cry. She had no answers but knew she had to go away to find out what had taken the light out of her heart and filled it with gloom and sadness. She was sure Symphony Hall would never invite her back but her agent, a great friend and confidante, assured Loretta that once she figured out what was going on, they would be thrilled to have her back. But first she needed to reflect on her past and everything that was going on in her life to comprehend why this had happened to her and how she could prevent it from happening again. Deep Lake House, she hoped, would help her understand why something inside her had died.

After her arrival at Deep Lake House, she barely left her room, choosing to observe the goings on at the House through her window. She planned to stay a month but as the weeks sped by and she relaxed and accepted her new fate as no longer a world-famous singer but simply a regular citizen, she began to venture out of her room. Her only hope was that no one would recognize her.

She had plenty of time during these several weeks to reflect on many things in her life, but mostly she thought about her mama who she'd lost when she was born. She felt cheated since she never got to know her. She remembered her Gran'mama telling her the most wonderful stories about her mama. She couldn't hear the stories enough and would beg gran'mama to tell her about the time her mama, when just a young girl, had walked right up to a policeman and asked if he would like a lollipop since she had two. She was the most generous child. So many of the stories brought tears to her gran'mama's eyes though, and she hesitated before asking gran'mama to tell them again. When she said she didn't want to make her sad, gran'mama gave the child a hug.

"Oh no, my sweet child. These are happy tears. I only have happy memories of your mama."

"But mama died, doesn't that make you sad?"

"Of course it does. But that is just one sad memory. Look at all the happy stories I've shared with you. So many. Why would I think only of the one sad story when there are so many happy ones?"

She also thought, over and over again, about her visit to the doctor when she could no longer sing. Her throat was a little red, irritated but there didn't appear to be any serious damage. Just a touch of laryngitis. She was singing a lot, perhaps she'd strained her voice and just needed a rest. That was when she had searched out and found Deep Lake House. She was positive this was just the cure she needed.

But there was a part of her that doubted the diagnosis. She had been singing for many years and had never 'strained' her voice. She was suspicious that it had to be something else. But she just couldn't imagine what it was.

Reminiscing was what she did mostly at Deep Lake House. So many memories brought smiles to her face that she felt all the way down to her toes. A warmth spread throughout as she relived so many special moments. These were the moments she tried to recall when the dark memories pushed their way into her thoughts. One such memory reappeared again and again, no matter how many happy ones she remembered, that she just couldn't chase out of her head. It was the night Alonzo came to her dressing room after a performance. The applause had gone on for so long she gave two encores. And then resting in her room, sipping a cool, sweet, and tart lemonade, a knock at her door brought her out of her relaxed state and back to reality. She was sure it was a fan who wanted to sing her praises. Or perhaps an agent who wanted to book her for yet another concert. She rarely had time to cool down after each concert before the fans began to line up. After meeting with several she would find her way out and into her waiting limo.

"Come in." She was sure it was Mr. Simonson, the stage manager, who would smother her with praise, but there was no response to her invite. Curious, she asked, "Who's there?"

"It's Alonzo."

She sat upright on her velvet-covered chaise lounge, unsure of what the voice had said.

"Alonzo?"

"Yes." The voice confirmed what she was sure she had not heard correctly.

"Come in." And she got up and walked toward the door as it opened. Standing in front of her was a man but all she saw was the boy who she knew as her older brother. When she had left home in her late teens, soon after gran'mama had passed away, she never looked back and never again spoke to Alonzo or her papa. She was sure neither of them was interested in anything Loretta did. Except maybe the money she was making. And as she wondered why it was that Alonzo now appeared at her dressing room door, she was sure that must be the reason and a coldness ran up her spine causing her to shiver.

"What can I do for you, Alonzo?"

"So formal. No hug for your long-lost brother?"

Loretta ignored the sarcasm and waited for the begging to start, convinced that was why he had sought her out. She had been giving concerts for years and Alonzo had never shown up before, so why now? It had to be for money.

"Ok, I'll get right to the point. But first, I know it has been years since we spoke, I have to tell you that even though this is the 1st time I've come to see you, I've tried my best to attend all of your concerts."

Loretta gasped, unsure of how to take this news. But again, just a prelude to the begging she was sure would come.

"You do know, I have no doubt, that you have such a beautiful voice. And I'm so happy for your success."

And now the obligatory flattery, Loretta thought, that was to be expected.

"I wish I had been brave when I was a boy and stood up to our papa. But I wasn't and for that I apologize. I guess that's one of the reasons I try to go to all of your concerts, whenever I can. To make up for my cowardice as a child."

Still, Loretta remained quiet, waiting.

"You have a niece, Elana, she is 5 now. Smart as a whip. I have a photo."

He opened his wallet and holding his arm out to Loretta, showed her the photo of a precious girl with two big front teeth and a smile as wide as her mouth could go, just as Loretta's was when she was a girl, and long almost black hair past her shoulders, again, like Loretta. Loretta felt a tear bubbling up in the corner of her eye.

"Her mother, my wife Sofia, cannot have any more children – and she must have a hysterectomy."

And, so, there it is. They need money for the operation. Again, Loretta waited.

"I'm an engineer, you know. I make very good money, we have a beautiful home. We wanted to have 3 or 4 children. But now. Anyway, I'm not sure why I'm telling you all this. I guess I was hoping you would want to meet them, my wife, Sophia, and our precious, Elana, your niece. Mostly though, and maybe you just don't care and I can't blame you if you don't but I wanted to tell you our father is failing. He has had 2 heart attacks and the doctors say he could not survive another. So, if you wanted to see him, now would be a good time.

And then Alonzo stopped speaking. And he waited.

Loretta, who now had two streams of tears running from her eyes, seemed unable to change the frozen, unemotional expression that had settled on her face from the moment she'd opened the door to see Alonzo standing in front of her.

"Do you have nothing to say, Loretta? If not, then I will leave now and wish you all the best and give you all my love. And say, again, I am sorry."

Still Loretta did not speak. Placing a card on a table as he backed out of the room, Alonzo made a slight bow, and then disappeared from sight.

Loretta quickly snapped out of her trance and stepping into the hallway, watching the back of her only brother walk away from her, said, "That is a surprise. I did not think papa had a heart."

Alonzo turned to face Loretta and nodding his head knowingly, turned to leave.

Back in Loretta's dressing room, the door locked, Loretta fell on her lounge chair and covering herself with a blanket, cried tears she had stored up in her body for the past 20 years.

She lay down for just a few minutes, exhausted by these memories that she relived too many times. Sleeping was the only way to escape these thoughts. But now she was sure hours had passed. The sun shone through the window, hitting her in the eyes, prying them open against her will. A quiet knock on the door forced them to open wide. She was sure it was Alonzo. But she suddenly recalled that had been months ago and she was at the Deep Lake House now, not in her dressing room where after her concert, Alonzo had come to talk to her about his family and about their father. Loretta pulled the cover up over her head. The soft knock again. She sat up, looked at the clock on the nightstand and saw that it was 3:30. But it wasn't ticking, so she realized she'd forgotten to wind it.

"Who's there?"

"Housekeeping, Miss Loretta. We've tried to come in to clean up for you but you have not been answering. Please let us come in and give you some clean sheets."

"What time is it?" She called out hoping the housekeeper was still there and hadn't left when she hesitated to answer.

A small voice answered. "It is 11:40, ma'am. They are serving lunch now in the dining room."

She decided then and there it was time to move, to get out of the bed, to face whatever this world at Deep Lake House had to offer her.

"Give me just 5 minutes, please."

"Yes, ma'am."

Loretta got up and went to her bathroom. A wash cloth and some soap would suffice for now. She threw on a loose shift and draped a sweater over her shoulders. She would have a light lunch in the dining room. When she opened the door, she was facing a young woman who couldn't have been more than 17. She stepped back, allowing the full-bodied diva to step out of the room. The girl averted her eyes. Loretta walked up to the girl and, lifting her chin, spoke directly to her.

"Stand tall, young one. Stand proud. Don't let anyone dictate your feelings to you. Be who you are meant to be, whatever path you pursue in life." And with that she continued on downstairs to the dining room.

The dining room was mostly empty; only two other tables were occupied, each seating two people. And at a third table a single woman sat, sipping a cup of tea, with a tea pot and small creamer pitcher next to her cup and saucer.

The woman appeared lost in her thoughts, her head bent down, looking up only briefly to pour her tea and add a little creamer. Loretta was sure she was a woman she had seen around the property a few times when she had been observing the goings on at Deep Lake House through her window. As she recalled, the woman had three children, a husband, and she guessed a mother-in-law who accompanied them on this vacation. The husband was leading the pack with the children running around his feet like a litter of puppies. The older woman stayed close behind. The younger woman, obviously the mother of the young children and who was now seated not far from Loretta, didn't seem to belong to the family that had walked ahead of her. Loretta knew people had their own troubles and felt for this woman, seeing the pained look that covered her face like a mask. But it was a mask that Loretta could see right through because she recognized it. It was her own face.

She watched the lone woman for a while, trying not to stare, but wanting to connect somehow. She was waiting for the right moment, and when the woman finally looked her way, Loretta didn't hesitate to draw her attention by humming a soft tune and opening her mouth just a bit to let the gentle notes flow out of her and over to the ears of the woman who responded with just the slightest smile. As the smile slowly spread across her face, Loretta took the opportunity to wave the woman to join her. As the woman's smile began to fade, and fearing she'd lost the sad woman, she pushed the chair closest to her out as an invitation and waved the waiter to her, instructing her to carry the woman's tea cup and saucer to Loretta's table. The woman then, only slightly reluctantly, stood up and slowly and carefully walked to Loretta's table and sat in the chair waiting for her.

Once the woman was situated with her tea pot, cup and saucer sitting in front of her, Loretta leaned in and looking deep into the woman's eyes, introduced herself.

"Hello, my name is Loretta Jordan. What's your name, hon?"

The woman stared into Loretta's kind and smiling eyes, wanting to linger as long as she could in the warmth and comfort she found there. Loretta was tempted to say the same inspiring words she gave to the 17-year-old girl just a short time ago. But this was a woman, a mother of three, not an awkward, shy teenager. A tear escaped and ran down the woman's face which she quickly wiped away with her napkin. Loretta waited patiently until the woman spoke. She appeared to be practicing what she would say and then she spoke in a hushed voice, that seemed unaccustomed to speaking out loud.

"My name is Mrs. Whitmore, Mrs. Samuel Whitmore." And then quickly correcting herself she said in a louder voice, "Eva, I'm Eva." She then extended a limp hand that Loretta grabbed in both of hers as if offering a rope to save the woman from drowning while hopefully transferring the love and warmth that flowed through her into Eva's cold hand. Another tear ran down Eva's cheek and again she wiped it away.

"It is very nice to meet you, Eva." Loretta let the woman's hand go and Eva, placing her hand in her lap, grasped it tightly with her other as if looking for another lifeline to hold onto.

"So, tell me Eva, are you here with your family, your husband, Samuel?"

Eva seemed surprised when Loretta mentioned Samuel, but then she remembered that she called herself 'Mrs. Samuel Whitmore.'

"Yes, yes I am." She smiled a little and looked away. Eva didn't mention her children.

"I know who you are." Eva blurted out, surprising Loretta with her boldness.

"Oh, ok." Loretta didn't know what else to say and waited for Eva to speak again.

"I saw you, in concert. You were marvelous, truly." Eva glowed with the memory of seeing Loretta on stage, perhaps seeing herself as a Diva, someone who strangers admired and praised for their unique and distinctive voice. Perhaps someone she also could have been, in another lifetime.

"Thank you so much for such high praise. I do appreciate it. I don't often get the opportunity to meet my fans and I do miss that connection. So, this is a special time for me, meeting you, Eva. I'm so happy to be here at Deep Lake House the same time you are here."

"How long are you staying? Is this just a vacation for a couple of weeks or a break from all of your concerts?" Eva was becoming more animated and opening up to Loretta. She seemed to relax right before Loretta's eyes and was smiling as Loretta shared with Eva how one night her voice just seemed to quit on her, right on stage. Eva was sympathetic and leaned in to Loretta, holding her hand as Loretta had done for Eva. Loretta could see the caring, soulful spirit that looked back at her and wondered how a man, an older woman, and three young children could be so distant from such an open, loving being. Loretta wanted to know more, but hesitated to ask too many questions fearing Eva might withdraw. She decided to keep the conversation light in the hopes that Eva would feel so comfortable she would just naturally share more about her life with Loretta.

"I've been doing all the talking now, what about you? Is this your first time at Deep Lake House or have you been coming here for years now?"

Eva pulled back as if remembering that she was actually here with her family. Her face changed, she seemed to hold her breath, as she looked quickly around the dining room.

"I should probably go. I've been here awhile. The children."

"Oh, do you have to? I'm enjoying our conversation so much. You see, I've been in my room for a couple of weeks now, haven't spoken to anyone until you. I'm feeling a bit lonely and am really grateful for your company."

Eva's face softened as she looked into Loretta's worried eyes. Eva seemed more relaxed when she was helping someone, taking the attention off of herself.

"I've been coming here several years now, for two weeks, is all, at a time. I have to get back to the city."

"Do you work, have a job that you have to get back to?" Loretta noticed how Eva didn't mention her family, only that she had to get back to the city. She wondered if she was talking about the past, before she had a husband and children in her life. Again, Eva's face changed as she retreated inward where some darkness continued to blanket whatever sunshine lived in her.

"No, not now. I did. I was a book editor. Now, I'm Mrs. Samuel Whitmore. That's all." A smile appeared for just a few seconds when she'd mentioned her previous job. But there was also a certain sadness within each word, causing Eva's head to drop forward.

"Well, that can be very rewarding as well, can't it? I mean, raising children is no easy task. I imagine it can be a full-time job." Eva kept her head lowered.

"Eva!" The voice echoed throughout the dining room, causing the wait staff as well as the other two parties to look at the small woman who was causing such a scene. And then the short rigid woman, dressed in black attire from head to foot, walked straight to Loretta's table. Eva had jumped at the sound of her name and stood up, turning to face the tyrant.

"What are you doing here and why are you talking to this woman? I thought you had a headache and needed to rest, or so you said. Or were you lying, again?" The woman barely reached Eva's chest and stood with her head back, staring, with stern mouth and black eyes, into Eva's face. Eva averted her eyes, stealing a mere glance at Loretta.

"Now just a minute here. We were having a cup of tea and enjoying each other's company. No need to shout." Loretta was appalled at the small woman's rude behavior and obvious abusive attitude towards Eva.

"Do I look like I'm talking to you? This is none of your concern so why don't you try minding your own business." Loretta felt her temper rising and knew what she wanted to say to this oppressor but feared the repercussions that would befall Eva.

"I think you should leave my table right now or I will call the management." Loretta caught one of the waiter's eyes and he quickly came to her aid.

"Excuse me, but you'll have to leave. You are disturbing our guests." The waiter felt helpless and hoped that would be enough to get the woman to leave.

Eva again glanced at Loretta and reaching out and touching her hand, said, "I'm so sorry. And thank you." And with that she ran off, the bully close on her heels.

Loretta sat, slowly shaking her head over what had just transpired, and called for her check.

Back in her room, Loretta worried about Eva. In a few short minutes, she had gotten a glimpse of what Eva's life must be like. An old woman like that could eat at your insides, causing ulcers or maybe even cancer to erupt. Loretta wished she could help Eva, but knew that unless Eva reached out to her, she would just be told, again, to mind her own business.

If felt good to focus on someone else's problems instead of her own for a change. Yes, she worried about her singing career and whether or not she would ever sing again. But she also felt the ache of knowing she had a niece she'd never met. A niece who she could be a real aunt to, a niece who she could visit and smother with gifts and love and maybe even introduce her to the world of the stage that Loretta knew so well. She might even be a singer someday. Loretta would help her, she could introduce Elana to all the right people, guide her, protect her from the swindlers who would surely take advantage of a young talent. That would never happen to her niece, Elana.

Suddenly, she began to feel an innate protectiveness for the only other person who would be as close to her as her own brother, and that was her brother's daughter, Elana. She knew at that moment that there was only one thing for her to do.

Without hesitation she sat at the desk in her room, pulled out the stationary provided by the House, and poured her heart out on that paper, recalling the visit from Alonzo just a few short months ago. A meeting she could never change, a meeting that now she wished had gone very differently. Alonzo apologized for his cowardice as a young boy, so many years ago. But Loretta somehow had felt a need to continue to punish him, knowing deep down it was her father who needed to be punished. She only hoped now that it wasn't too late. A young girl's life was at stake, her niece, Elana. Loretta knew her life, also, was at stake. She would be the aunt Elana needed, she would be a part of her life, now until Loretta's end. She would make time in her schedule to mentor the young girl, if Alonzo and his wife, Sophia, allowed. She would bring Alana to her concerts, as many as she could. And she would join Alonzo's family at every holiday, if they would have her, if it wasn't too late.

Loretta quickly finished her letter and hurried downstairs to get it into the outgoing mail. She knew it would take a while before Alonzo would receive it. She was happy he had taken the time to write down his address for her, perhaps he was hoping she would eventually come to her senses. Back in her room, an emotionally exhausting afternoon earned her a nap.

When Loretta woke, she felt refreshed, like a new woman! She knew it had to do with the burden she had been carrying around with her for so long. And just like that she felt lighter, the weight was gone. She took a bath and decided she needed to go downstairs to dinner, to meet other people, to open her heart even wider and allow others in, to let the joy that was now in her heart, in her soul, flow through her and send it outward to others, to spread it far and wide. That was who she really was, that was the real Loretta, the one who could spread love through her singing.

Once out of the tub and dressed, Loretta was excited to see who she might meet at dinner. She hoped she would see Eva there and this time she would stand taller for the woman, set an example for the woman who needed help standing up for herself. She would do what she could to get her away from all of them, even paying for her fare to get back to the city, to help her find work doing what Eva loved, working as a book editor and maybe even writing her own book, if that was what she wanted. For the first time in a long time, Loretta was feeling useful and helpful. She was sure she was on the road to recovery now. She began to hum, testing out her voice, positive that now it would come back since the tension she'd been holding inside her was gone.

Loretta entered the dining room that was filled with the buzzing of soft-spoken words and a somber energy. She looked around for a waiter to seat her but they were all standing in a group, their heads down, whispering amongst themselves and seemingly unable to move from where they stood, needing the support and strength of their fellow waiters. Miss Loretta walked to the group and quietly asked what was happening, intuiting that something was not at all right. The older girl, one who had waited on Miss Loretta several times and had brought up her meals to her room, stepped forward.

"There has been a drowning. The sheriff said they just found the body."

"A death? Oh my, how awful. Do they know who it is? Was it someone who was staying here at Deep Lake House?" A feeling of sadness sent shivers all over Miss Loretta's skin. She already knew the answer to her question.

The wait staff looked to the desk clerk who was walking towards them. He whispered to the group and a couple of them, the younger ones, put their hands to their mouths, horrified at the news, and one young girl began to cry while a couple of the others comforted her. The older girl turned back to Miss Loretta.

"It was Mrs. Samuel Whitmore."

"You mean, Eva. It was Eva Whitmore?" Miss Loretta felt the need to acknowledge that Eva was her own person, not an extension of Mr. Samuel Whitmore. It was with a great deal of willpower that Miss Loretta walked out of the room and back to her own room, holding in a great wall of tears.

How quickly a life, a living, breathing human life, the heart beating, the lungs filling with air, blood pumping through the veins, can, just like that, come to a complete and final stop, an end, never to beat, or breathe, or pump again. Loretta more than once, found herself in awe of how precious life, our lives, were. It was just a few short hours ago that she had been speaking to Eva and now Eva was forever gone. Why didn't Loretta do more? Could she have done more? She knew the woman was in pain. Or was it all, only, in Eva's hands? The only one who was truly in charge. Not even Samuel or the wretched mother-in-law had a role in Eva's death. Only Eva could have decided to take this one final step. Only Eva could allow, Loretta stopped at this word, allow, because that is what Eva had done, she allowed these people who had no interest in her well-being, who seemed to be there only to drive Eva deeper and deeper into misery, do so until she couldn't bear it any longer. Yes, Eva allowed them to control her thoughts and ultimately her actions, giving them all the power. She allowed this to happen. Why? Because she was too weak to fight them all. But with no one on her side, where would she have gotten her strength? Would any of them miss her? The children? Loretta wondered if the children, the innocent ones, felt any love for their mother. Or had they been turned against her as well? Her own children who she had given birth to.

But was it truly only Eva's fault? Now Loretta felt guilty for blaming the woman who was so tortured by her family for her own death. Would she have taken her life otherwise if she hadn't felt as though there was no way out of her situation? The others, her mother-in-law and her husband mostly, because children are innocent in their decisions when they are controlled by an adult, ultimately drove Eva to a point where she was out of options. Her mother-in-law wanted Eva gone. Her husband left everything up to his mother. She had no support. Her children were basically estranged from her. She was alone.

Loretta was so happy she had given Eva her time and wished she had done something more, anything, to help Eva. But what could she have possibly done? Maybe if she'd had more time with Eva. But she had just met her, and now she was gone. Maybe Loretta didn't meet Eva to help her, maybe Eva was already gone when they met. Maybe Loretta was the one who needed help to live, to change, to open her heart to others, to her own family, and welcome them in. Perhaps this was a lesson Loretta needed to learn; how fast time goes, how we are here and then we are gone. And how would Loretta feel, knowing that she has a niece and a brother who wants her in his life and wants his daughter to know her aunt, if suddenly Loretta was gone, or her brother, or her niece? She now knew that she had to completely let go of the anger she was still holding inside against her father and how he had treated her when she was a child. For that was in the past and she would never be able to change the past.

But she could change the future. The future wasn't here yet, she could have a new life with her brother's family. With her family. Suddenly, waiting for Alonzo to receive her letter was no longer an option. She ran down to the front desk, asked to place a call, and checking the number Alonzo had written down with his address, dialed. The phone was picked up after the 2nd ring.

"Alonzo, this is Loretta. I'm coming home."

Maisy Tuttle

(1950s)

.

Chapter 7

A frail, gentle young woman, pretty in a petite way with short, deep reddish hair the color of acorns, there were none to compare to Maisy. You get a special feeling from some people immediately and that was how I felt the first time I saw Maisy Tuttle. I wanted her to feel as if she was home. I wanted her to enjoy the peace and serenity that my walls exuded. I wanted her to smile and unload the burden she seemed to carry on her back. I wanted her to stay forever. But I knew that was not possible, no one ever does. They shared their lives for a week or two, maybe a month and then they were gone, many to return the following year and some for many years after that. But Maisy, I wanted her to stay. She brought such joy to those who met her – she always had a smile, taking your hand in both of hers like a hug. Your hand didn't want to be let go and would linger as long as she allowed. You felt like it was just you and her in the world.

It was the mid-1950s and the walls in her room at that time were covered in a pattern of red and yellow roses, entwined with baby's breath throughout. The welcoming sunlight danced across the wooden floors when the sheer pink curtains parted and rejoined as the breeze blew through the open windows. It was my favorite room. She would run her hand over the flowers on my walls, tracing the patterns as if they were real, caressing the velvet-like petals. She seemed to be the only one who noticed the curtains breathing in the fresh air and spent much time in front of the windows, staring out into the lake, sometimes even at night.

Each year Maisy came she stayed for two weeks. She would walk down to the beach area, a book in her hand, and sit in one of the lounge chairs that the house provided to its guests. Sometimes she kept her nose in her book, turning page after page, never looking up. Other times she never opened the book at all. She would find something in the distance across the lake and stare at it, transfixed as if in a hypnotic state. I'm sure only

Maisy knew what held her attention so strongly. And then after several hours, the sun lowering itself to the horizon, she would come back from wherever she had gone, close her book if she had been reading it, get up from the lounge chair and walk back to her room. The times she stared out across the lake she walked much slower, as if she hadn't completely come back from wherever it was she had gone.

She dined alone with a book her only companion. For six years Maisy Tuttle's life at Deep Lake House proceeded in the same way. She never brought a guest, neither male nor female. Like many of our guests who came alone, she seemed to prefer her own company. Of course, she always brought fictional friends, characters who lived in the pages of the books she read. She often laughed out loud after reading a passage. Or she'd close the book and bring a tissue to the corners of her eyes. Or she would close the book, look out across the lake, her view from her room's bay window, and stand there until the clock in the downstairs entryway had passed two hours. I can still see her picking up a pen and rapidly writing until her pen ran out of ink or her hand started to cramp. She always carried an ample supply in a canvas bag along with notebooks. By the looks of it, these were more often working vacations for Maisy Tuttle than relaxing ones.

The excitement she exhibited seemed to vibrate off her creating a glow as the ideas raced down to her fingers and out through her pen as she tried desperately to get every word inside her onto paper, apparently fearful that she might lose them before she got them all out. Lost in her world, her face flush, she paused only long enough to shake her cramped hand and slap it into submission and kept writing. By the time she had finished getting all of her words out, she was drained, falling onto her bed, napping for more than an hour. With this vacation turning into yet another working one, it was obvious she was leaving nearly as tense as when she had arrived.

For six years this has been her routine. Whether or not it was fulfilling no one but Maisy knew for sure. But in her seventh year, everything changed. She never really shared her life. And strangely, no one asked. But she would listen to whoever wanted to share their story. A good listener, she had been taught, when she was a child, that no adult was interested in what a child had to say. She somehow didn't recognize that she, too, was now an adult and she had a life that was at least as interesting as any of the others with whom she'd spend hours of her life listening to their story. But as an editor, she was used to reading stories so listening to others talk about their lives felt like the same thing. It felt like her job. People filled her with ideas, too, that helped to shape her poems. She had written close to two hundred and hoped one day to put them into a book. If she had time.

Maisy seemed exceptionally tired when she arrived for her 7th year. She spent several days relaxing and resting in her room, reading and writing, her usual entertainments, and walking to the beach and enjoying the sun. With just a few days left to her vacation, she came down to the dining room before they were ready to serve dinner and ordered a cup of tea. She came empty-handed, carrying only a small book of poems, which seemed to be all she could manage. Sitting alone at a corner table, she focused on the wall paper pattern, similar to the wall paper in her room except these were clusters of magnolia flowers interwoven with baby's breath. But with the same raised velvety pattern. She traced each individual flower with her eyes. So engrossed in this task was she that she never heard the man who spoke to her three times. When she finally did hear someone, it was a voice, almost as soft as her own but far deeper.

"Excuse me, Miss, may I join you? Of course, if you are waiting for someone then I'll find myself another seat. Or if you prefer to sit alone…"

Maisy looked up, startled, staring boldly into the eyes of the man who stood before her, taking him in as if sizing him up for a new suit of clothes. It took her only seconds to snap out of her reverie, but to him it felt like several long minutes had passed.

"I'm so sorry, what did you say?"

"Oh, no need to apologize. I interrupted you, please accept my apology. I was wondering, since we seem to be the only two guests, if you wanted some company. But since you seem to be content in your own thoughts, perhaps I should leave you to them and, again, apologize for my awkward and insensitive intrusion."

The man started to back away, not even giving Maisy a chance to agree with or reject his assumptions.

"Certainly not the most flattering invitation I've ever had, but definitely the longest apology."

The young man stepped forward again, smiling and blushing.

"So, is that a yes?"

"Yes, that would be fine. My thoughts too often take me to places I'd rather not go anyway, so I welcome a distraction of any kind."

"Touché."

"Excuse me."

"Not the most flattering invitation I've ever had."

Maisy smiled her sweetest smile and pointed to the chair to her left.

As soon as he sat down, he extended his right hand and introduced himself.

"I'm Mitchell Stewart, delighted to meet you."

Maisy extended her right hand which was immediately taken into both of his. Their warmth was comforting, like a warm bath surrounding her, and she felt a strong desire to close her eyes and nap. And then she realized how others might feel since she greeted many the same way, with both hands. But she quickly composed herself and slowly withdrew her hand from his two strong, yet gentle, hands.

"Maisy, Maisy Tuttle. Pleased to meet you, Mitchell."

A waiter walked towards them carrying a tray. He placed the teapot, cup and saucer, spoon and a selection of tea in front of Mitchell.

"More hot water, Miss?"

"Yes, please." Maisy handed Robert, the waiter, her empty pot.

"So, Maisy, what brings you to Deep Lake House?"

"Well, I've been coming here each year for two weeks for... well, this is my 7th year."

"This is my 3rd year. How is it we've never met?"

"I don't know. I do spend a lot of time in my room or down at the beach. And when I do eat here in the dining room, my dining companion is usually the latest book I'm reading. Also, this isn't my usual time of year to visit Deep Lake House. I usually come in the fall, September or October."

"That would explain it. I always come here in May before the families arrive. I like the quiet and how everything is just starting to bloom, nature is so fragile at this time of year, vulnerable to the weather and late snows, but still it pushes through, becoming what it is meant to be."

"Very poetic, Mitchell."

"Well, I am a writer. Actually, an engineer by trade, but that's just to pay the bills, put aside some savings, that sort of thing. Writing is my passion. If I could make a living at it, that is all I would do. And that's why I come to Deep Lake House. To write. That's my sole purpose for coming here and also why I come at a more quiet, less busy time of year."

"I also enjoy the quiet and I enjoy the less-crowded time of year that fall offers. Plus, the trees, the colors, I never tire of that and find myself easily transported to another time." Maisy gazed off into the distance, as if to demonstrate.

"So, are you a writer, also?"

"Poetry mostly. But it is more of a hobby, I guess."

"Well, Maisy, I would love to read some, if you care to share. How many have you written?"

"More than 200 now, I think."

"Two hundred? That's more than just a hobby. You, my dear, are a poet."

The waiter returned with the hot water and placed it to Maisy's right, without disturbing the couple. Maisy caught his eye and gave him a nod and a smile.

Maisy, returning her attention to Mitchell and thinking about the generous compliment he'd just given her, smiled brightly at the young man. His enthusiasm was contagious. She knew she was a poet, she just wasn't sure if she was ready to share this knowledge with the world. Although starting small, sharing just with Mitchell, was probably a good start.

"Is that how you make your money, Maisy, I mean to pay the bills and for food? You know what, that's way too personal. Sorry. I ask a lot of questions. I guess I have my writer's hat on. Sorry."

"It's ok. I don't mind if you ask questions. That's how you find out about someone, if you want to get to know them. So, I'll ask you one. What's your novel about?"

Mitchell's face lit up and a smile spread across his face. Maisy knew she had asked the right question.

"Without going into too much detail, it's a kind of love story. Of course, I always hear you should write what you know. I know engineering, science, you know, really technical stuff. But who wants to read about that? So, I had to go into my heart and that's where I found what I really wanted to write about. Love. I know it sounds corny, a guy writing romance novels. I guess I'm following in the footsteps of Samuel Taylor Coleridge. And of course, there's Shakespeare, Tolstoy, and Dickens. That's pretty good company. And you know the familiar story line, boy meets girl, they fall in love, and then one of them dies of a terminal illness."

"Maybe you shouldn't divulge too much of your novel to me. You really shouldn't talk about it until it's completed. That is, if you are paranoid the story might be stolen by another writer. But maybe, just to be safe, you should wait until it's finished before sharing it."

"Ok, it's a deal. But I would like to ask you another question."

"Sure."

"What are you doing for dinner? If you aren't too attached to a novel at this point, perhaps I could be your dinner partner tonight?"

"I would really like that."

Back in her room, Maisy was suddenly flustered, unsure of what to wear. She started to rethink her decision to meet Mitchell for dinner and thought she should call his room and cancel. Just tell him she wasn't feeling well. He'll understand. She has a headache, she's busy packing and needs to rest as she's tired, but maybe tomorrow they could dine. Or maybe not call at all and just avoid seeing him again. Or tell him the next day she fell asleep and then avoid the dining room and eat in her room like she usually did. The more she thought about it the more it seemed like a good plan. But for the remainder of her stay? She would have to avoid running into him for the next several days. But what if he searched her out? It was quiet, they may be the only two guests at the House for all she knew. Did she tell him her room number? She couldn't remember. But he could easily find it out. Everyone knew her at the House, someone would tell him. She could see no way around it – she would have to meet Mitchell for dinner.

She suddenly realized how ridiculous she must sound if her thoughts were spoken out loud. A handsome, intelligent young man had asked her to dinner and she was trying to find an excuse, any excuse, not to meet him for dinner. But it was more than that. It wasn't just dinner. It was what might happen during dinner or in the next few days. One or both of them may fall in love. And that just could not happen.

She did like him and found herself smiling just now as she thought about him. He was a very likeable man and she enjoyed talking with him. She also really liked his face; it was a happy face, open and inviting, like he was ready for whatever came his way and he would not allow anything negative in. She couldn't envision him angry or arguing about whatever didn't really matter in life; he didn't have the time to expend any energy in that way. He was upbeat and positive and always would be. He would make some woman a great partner, supporting her in whatever path she took. If she wanted to be a mother, he would support that decision and would be the best father a child could hope for. If she wanted, instead, to pursue a career he would support her every choice, knowing that she had her own life to live. Whichever woman he married. She didn't know how she could see these character traits in him after just having met and spending less than an hour together but somehow, she felt sure she was right.

Time was ticking away and she needed to get ready for dinner. She bathed and quickly put on one of the few dresses she'd brought for this stay; a blue and white polka dot shift with a black patent leather belt. She added a black cardigan and after fluffing her hair with her fingers, adding a dot of color to her pale cheeks, and a soft tangerine lipstick, she was ready to go. She shut off the part of her brain that questioned her every move and decided to enjoy having dinner with a handsome young man whose conversation she found both stimulating and pleasant. She thought about their conversation earlier that day and how she couldn't help but smile as he shared his excitement about whatever subject they were discussing. He had been almost like a child with a shiny new toy on Christmas morning.

At five minutes to 5 she left her room and walked down the hallway towards the dining room. She knew that she could turn and walk back to her room, feigning an illness so as not to disappoint Mitchell too much. This dinner date could only lead to more time together and ultimately an unhappy ending. He was such a sweet man, she wanted to treat him fairly and honestly. But time would go by quickly and then they would be back to their own lives, far away from each other in different parts of the country, although she had no idea where he lived. But it didn't matter, she really didn't see the point.

And then she saw Mitchell standing in front of the door leading into the dining room. She saw him shift his weight from one foot to the other, checking his watch each time. She never saw a young man look so distraught waiting for his date to show up, but she was glad she had this opportunity. She couldn't help but smile as she walked towards him and saw how his face lit up when he looked up and saw her walking towards him. Thrusting the flowers out towards her was the final gesture that clinched it for Maisy – she was in love. Not the feeling she was looking to develop during her two weeks at Deep Lake House, but there it was. She hadn't felt this way in so long, she almost didn't recognize it. And if anyone had asked, even now when she'd admitted it to herself, she would strongly deny it.

She took the bouquet and felt the color rush to her face, feeling as young and inexperienced in dating as Mitchell's gestures seemed to reveal about him. Two adults acting like two teenagers on a first date. To an outsider, Maisy was sure they looked silly. Always proper in her appearance and movements, she suddenly felt awkward and terribly uncoordinated, even stumbling when they were being seated at their table. And Mitchell, the perfect gentleman, having pulled back her chair, offered his arm to prevent her from falling. She felt the strength in his forearm and again, felt a tingling in her cheeks.

They both looked over the menu and made their selections quickly. Mitchell ordered a burgundy wine for himself and when he asked Maisy what she might want to drink, she shook her head. Mitchell seemed anxious to speak but waited for the waiter to leave.

"I'm so glad you did not cancel; I was afraid you might." Mitchell's honesty was refreshing and at the same time, surprising. Most young men would not admit their vulnerabilities to a young woman, especially on their first date. Maisy decided not to share her indecision about whether or not to join him for dinner. He was genuinely happy to see her so she decided she wouldn't do anything to disappoint him.

"I'm happy that I came, also."

Their conversation continued about books and Mitchell had questions, wanting to know about Maisy. Although the personal questions that Mitchell brought up almost ended their night early, Maisy decided she liked Mitchell even more now and wanted to continue talking with him. But she thought it was best not to share anything too personal with him since, after all, they very likely would never see each other again. Maisy feared she would say something in reference to their possibility of a future together so she tread carefully and instead thought it best to bring their conversation, and all future conversations, however many that may be, back to books.

Dinner over, they walked back to their rooms. Maisy was surprised to see that the time was nearly 11:30 – she hoped Mitchell, who insisted on paying, had tipped Robert sufficiently since he'd waited for them while they had continued their conversation, oblivious to their surroundings until they had been the only ones in the dining room for at least two hours. The House was not full and although there had been three other couples for dinner, Maisy and Mitchell had stayed well beyond closing time.

Despite a rocky start to their conversation that evening, it had turned out to be most enjoyable and Maisy was very happy she had decided to join Mitchell for dinner. Of course, she could tell he was falling for her and she was already smitten. She knew this was a mistake and she really should end it. But since she would be leaving in just a couple of days, she tried to convince herself that having dinner or breakfast with a handsome young man and enjoying conversation, when she usually spent most of her time at the House alone in her room, was just what she needed.

Once they reached her door, Maisy knew Mitchell wanted a kiss. She wasn't sure what she wanted but he was the perfect gentleman and would only do what Maisy allowed. And just like that she let Mitchell kiss her; or rather, she kissed him. He was bending to her cheek while holding her hand and she decided she wanted to feel his lips on hers. And just as she'd imagined, they were as warm and comforting as his hands had been when he'd held hers at tea. He wrapped his other arm around her and the embrace felt somehow familiar. It felt like Deep Lake House, a place where you wanted to stay forever and wondered how you could have survived without it all these years. But Maisy knew this was just wishful thinking and, pulling herself away, she backed into her room leaving the sweet man standing alone in the hallway in front of her door.

Once in her room, she relived the wonderful evening they'd had, leaving out the past memories that had nearly spoiled their delightful dinner. She wished she could let those memories go but she no longer felt anger and sadness towards the man she'd nearly married. Most of that anger inside her now was for how she'd deceived herself. She'd spent more than a normal amount of time wondering how she could not have known. Or had she and she just refused to see it? She'd been so sure David was the one, so positive they would grow old together. So certain about everything, and now she doubted every decision she made, wondering if it was the wrong one. Because, after all, she'd thought she was right about everything with David and then when she'd found out the truth, she wondered what other wrong decisions she had made in life and didn't trust herself to make the right ones anymore. How could she be so wrong?

But it no longer mattered, nothing mattered. Just finishing her editing and maybe getting her poems into a book. That would be her legacy. And that would be enough.

The next day Maisy checked out, just a couple of days early, leaving without saying good-bye to Mitchell. She knew this was for the best.

Mitchell Stewart

(1950s)

Chapter 8

The very second Mitchell Stewart walked through the double doors at Deep Lake House, I knew this was a special young man. Tall and slim with a neatly trimmed head of dark hair, he wore a suede jacket, a red and white plaid flannel shirt, and a pair of black chinos. His shoes served more than one purpose, with the most important one being they were comfortable for long walks. But the most striking thing about him was the smile that graced his face and lit up like a sunbeam following him to the front desk.

Vera Sundstrom, at the desk, had been expecting the young man to show up sometime that morning. She found herself unable to look away, her eyes following him as he approached, and her smile mirrored the one on his face as she greeted him.

"Hello, and how may I help you today? Or maybe I should ask, are you Mr. Stewart?" Vera, having spent more than 40 years at the House, greeted every guest with the same polite enthusiasm, never losing her kind, friendly manner in all those years.

"Hello to you! What a lovely place this is. You know, a friend told me about Deep Lake House and suggested I stay here. And so far, I'm quite taken with it." He turned, surveying the great room with eyes full of wonder taking in the rustic log walls, wide barn board floors, and the grand stone fireplace gracing the far wall. Completing his visual tour, Mitchell wound up facing the desk with Vera seemingly just as mesmerized with the young man as he was with the House.

"I'm terribly sorry, yes, Mitchell Stewart and I've reserved a room for 2 weeks at your magnificent Inn, I mean, House. So sorry."

"Oh, no, no, please, no reason at all to apologize. I'm thrilled that you are here and pleased that our House has made such a favorable first impression. Welcome. Yes, I see you are in Room 2B, Mr. Stewart."

"Please, call me Mitchell, or Mitch. I'm not one for formalities."

"And I see you've prepaid for the room so you will only need to pay for meals or souvenirs, that sort of thing. Your room is on the 2nd floor, take the stairs to your left and take a right at the top. Do you need any help with your luggage?"

"Oh no, I'm fine, I travel light. Now, just to confirm, that is a room at the end, correct? I did request a room with only one room adjacent, for the quiet you see. I'm here to write."

"Oh, yes, of course, no problem, sir, um, Mitch, there are no other guests at that end and let me see, no, no one else next week as well. You'll have that entire corner of the House to yourself, so you'll have all the peace and quiet you want."

"Perfect!"

"Do you have any other questions? I have some brochures of the area's attractions, if you're interested. You've said you're here to write, but if you take some time for other activities, there are some local places of interest."

"Hiking, I do like a good hike. You have lots of land to hike, I did see that in your brochure. 110 acres, was it? I find it clears the head for writing."

"Yes, exactly right, 110 acres and there is also a wildlife reserve abutting our land with over 300 acres, so there's plenty of hiking trails."

"Any hunting?"

"Oh, no, there's no hunting allowed on the property or on the wildlife reserve, either."

"Perfect."

"So, any more questions, Mitchell, Mitch?"

"Just one, are you the owner, Vera? I see your name tag has only your name."

"No, not me. Mr. Lloyd Cummings, real estate broker in New York, he's the owner now. We've had a couple of owners over the years. If you're interested in the House's history, we have lots of photos and information around the house that make a lovely self-guided tour. I think you would enjoy it."

"That sounds wonderful, I'll do that. And I'll have to write to Mr. Cummings when I return home and tell him how beautiful his House is."

"Well, you can write to him and drop a letter in the box right here on the desk. We send him mail weekly and if you write your return address, he'll answer your letter. There's stationary in your room if you'd care to write a letter."

Mitchell's first 2-week stay at Deep Lake House went by faster than he expected and he wished he could've stayed on for another two weeks. He made the best progress he'd made thus far on his novel and wanted to continue working on it, but it was time to get back to reality and his full-time job. Before he left, he did drop a note in the box for Lloyd Cummings thanking him for making his two weeks the best experience he'd had on a vacation. And then he booked the same room for the same two weeks next year.

Before he left, he bought Vera a bouquet of tulips and thanked her for all of her kindnesses to him. Even though she had only just met the young man, she couldn't stop the one tear from running down her cheek, blushing as she took the young man's thoughtful gift, wishing she had a daughter she could match him up with. But Vera and her late husband, Ivan, only had a son who'd married and moved to Sweden with his wife and two daughters. Her son, Sven, had lived in Sweden for only a few years when he was a child, before they had moved to the States. Vera only saw them every 3 or 4 years. Now that she was getting older, she thought about retiring soon and moving back to Sweden to be near her son and his family. But the House and all the employees had become a 2nd family for her. And occasionally she met a guest like Mitchell who made her life at the House worthwhile, knowing the work she was doing was having such a positive effect on the guests who came to stay.

And now Mitchell was here for his 3rd year. His book was nearly complete even though he had very little time at home to work on it with his full-time job and volunteer commitments.

He had also begun looking for a house, having tired of the apartment lifestyle and influenced by the peace and quiet of life at Deep Lake House. He was hoping these two weeks at the House would allow him to finish up the novel and also send out a few letters to potential publishers.

There was another clerk at the desk when Mitchell arrived. He hoped Vera was ok and asked about her.

"Is Vera still working here?"

"Oh yes, but she's on holiday. She should be back next week. She went to visit her son and his family in Sweden."

"Oh, fantastic. She'll have stories to tell then when she returns."

"Do you know Vera well?"

"Only from having stayed here – this is my 3rd year. She's part of what makes this place so special." The young man behind the desk, his badge said "James", nodded his head the entire time Mitchell was talking. His smile said it all and Mitchell could tell James agreed completely. Of course, he didn't expect anything else. They certainly wouldn't hire someone who was moody or unfriendly.

"Oh yes, I agree. Vera's the best. This is only my first year here, I started last fall, but she's been wonderful and so helpful to me. I hope they like me and I can stay on for many years."

Mitchell thought maybe Vera was thinking of retiring and so needed to find a replacement. Of course, she wouldn't tell James that but he was sure Mr. Cummings knew.

He signed in for his regular room; again, there were no other guests staying next to him and he appreciated the quiet. He was sure he'd be able to finish his book this time.

Mitchell didn't date much due to lack of time and his commitment to his writing. He was the guy who was there first thing in the morning and often the last to leave at night. Although, in reality, he wasn't always staying late for his job. Sometimes, having cleaned up his desk for the day and ready to head home, an idea for his novel would pop into his head and he would start writing. Hours would pass before he realized it was dark outside and he hadn't eaten supper, yet. He liked his job enough, but what he really wanted was to be a writer. So, if that meant making sacrifices to get to the place where he could finally quit his job, then he would do whatever it took to make that happen. He'd read about other authors working at jobs until they got a book published and then maybe working part time until their writing caught on. He knew it was possible and so put 110% into his writing.

And now he was excited to be back at the place where he'd always made so much progress with his writing and knew this was the year when he'd finally finish his first novel. He'd contacted a couple of publishing houses, but so far hadn't received any positive responses. He knew it didn't happen overnight and that you just had to keep sending your novel out. He wouldn't give up. Whenever he thought about having his book published, an energy surged through his body, giving him renewed hope to keep going. He just knew he was on the right path and at the right place at the right time. This magical place, Deep Lake House, was where he would finish his novel. He was sure of it.

After unpacking, Mitchell decided to go down to the dining room to see if he could get a cup of tea and maybe a bite to eat. It was too early for dinner, but at this point he would accept whatever they had.

Entering the dining room he looked around, first at the great fireplace at the far wall and then at the tables, various sizes to accommodate large or small parties, for a place to sit. The place was empty except for one table where a young woman sat alone. She was staring at the wall beside her, not at the book on the table in front of her. She had a pot of tea, so Mitchell was encouraged. Mitchell gestured to a waiter who had just come into the dining room and when he approached, Mitchell requested tea. The waiter turned and left without disturbing the young lady.

The woman was obviously deep in thought and Mitchell hesitated to disturb her. But he was really looking for some company right now, and a young, attractive woman would be perfect. He'd always enjoyed the company of women more than men. Women were much more poetic and open, willing to share their feelings with whoever would listen and far better at listening. Men were guarded, fearful of personal questions, and suspicious of your reasons should you ask anything about their feelings. Mitchell sometimes wondered if he would have been happier as a psychologist. He was so interested in the feelings that made someone weep or express anger. Because it was these things he needed to know to become a better writer.

He slowly approached the woman, not wanting to startle her, and ever so quietly asked if he could join her. The face that looked up at him was as perfect as he had ever seen; the smooth and flawless complexion was like that of the finest porcelain dolls he'd seen in China. He'd traveled there once for business and had bought his favorite niece a China doll. He'd bought the doll after reading about how the artists made them using only their hands for tools. He was amazed at how smooth the dolls' faces were, that anyone could create such magnificent dolls using only their hands. His niece had been enchanted and after putting the doll in a special place on her shelf next to her other dolls, had hugged him while whispering this would always be her favorite doll. She named it Su Lee. The doll stood out among the others with its red dragon patterned kimono, tiny slippered feet, and holding a red and gold fan. It was true, the doll did seem to command more attention than her other plastic-figured dolls with their plaid and floral dresses.

But this woman, with the brightest blue eyes, the Cupid's bow lips with just a touch of pink color, and a bit of a button nose, all framed by the deepest reddish brown short hair, stopped Mitchell in his tracks and he was almost unable to continue with his request to sit with her. She was surprisingly cordial and friendly, however, and within minutes Mitchell found himself joining her for tea.

Their too-brief conversation, lasting only as long as it took to finish a pot of tea, ended before Mitchell would have liked and so, without thinking, he asked Maisy to join him for dinner.

He was thinking, after she'd accepted, that their 5 o'clock dinner date could not get here fast enough.

He watched her walk away from him and felt a pull at his heart. There was something about her that he just couldn't pinpoint but he knew he was supposed to be with her. How could this happen? How could he have fallen head over heels in love in just an hour? But he did know something about love. That is why he chose to write about it. He'd fallen in love as a teenager and also had his heart broken at that tender age. He'd thought that it was forever when you found the right one. But now, years later, he realized that if the young girl he'd met as a teen had been the right one, it never would have ended. He and Sylvia had been together for two years. But when he'd seen her kissing his best friend, he thought his world would end right then and there. He wouldn't allow anyone to do that to him again and thought he couldn't ever trust another woman. So, all through college he focused only on his studies, graduating summa cum laude, 1st in his class in Engineering. He had protected himself for so long from his feelings that he felt empty inside. When he got a job, he started to open up again and allowed himself to get close to a couple of women, because feeling something was better than the hollow feeling he'd felt in his heart for so many years. But none of them had reached him in the way Maisy did. As they talked, he'd felt his heart opening up more than he'd ever imagined was possible. And his feelings now were those of an adult, not the puppy love he'd had with Sylvia so many years ago.

Even though he had less than an hour to prepare for dinner with Maisy, he wanted to show her how much he appreciated her company and decided to pick some wildflowers for her. He'd been taught that when you date a woman for the first time, you should always bring a gift. He really didn't think a gift would be appropriate since this wasn't a planned date but an impromptu one, but he thought a bouquet of wildflowers would be perfect. There would be plenty more opportunities to shower her with gifts, he was quite sure. Not wanting to get too far ahead of himself in planning their lives together, he walked out the front door and down to the beach area and then into the woods, searching for whatever wildflowers he could find.

Finally, having found enough of a variety to pass for a bouquet, Mitchell walked back to the House. After asking nicely for a piece of wet napkin and a sheet of aluminum foil to wrap around the bouquet, he went back to his room to get ready for his date with Maisy.

Fortunately, he'd brought a couple of dress shirts, just in case he decided to have a nice dinner in the dining room. He always felt he was honoring a restaurant by dressing up rather than dressing casually. They took the time to present you with a table that was covered with a clean cloth, heavy silverware, and sometimes fresh flowers in a vase, so the least he could do was dress equally fine as a way of saying thanks. He was able to dress a little more casual at work, taking off his tweed sports coat when he arrived at his office. But he did always wear a white, blue, or yellow button-down Oxford shirt with a tie. It was required dress. His pants were dress chinos. He never wore a hat although a lot of men where he worked did. He liked to feel the sun and air on his head. In the winter he wore a jacket with a hood.

Mitchell dressed quickly and was ready with 10 minutes to spare before the time they'd set, five o'clock, when the dining room opened. He considered asking at the front desk for her room number so he could call on her. But then he thought he'd better not – she might need some extra time to get ready and not want to feel rushed. Yes, he decided it was better to just wait. He checked his appearance in the mirror one last time and decided he was ready. Taking the bouquet he'd so carefully put together, he left his room and headed down to the dining room.

Mitchell paced in front of the dining room's door, glancing up to see if Maisy was coming his way. The House wasn't in full capacity, far from it, so only two waiters were serving that evening. And of course, the very prompt Mitchell was the first to arrive. What seemed like hours was only ten minutes when

Maisy was walking toward Mitchell. His hands clutched the bouquet and he thrust it forward, feeling like a schoolboy gifting his teacher with a shiny apple. He blushed as the stunning figure of Maisy, all smiles, reached for the bouquet. He was happy to release the sweaty foil and quickly wiped his hands down his pant legs.

"You look beautiful, Maisy."

"Thank you so much, Mitchell." Maisy couldn't hide her pleasure at such an honest and spontaneous compliment.

"These are lovely, Mitchell. But where did you find them? I didn't think there were any flowers around yet, it's kind of early for flowers around here."

"Well, I did look high and low. But they have a garden here on the property and James at the front desk, told me I could look there because sometimes a few different flowers bloom early. But I mostly found everything just walking around through the woods. I also enjoyed a pleasant, although brief, walk on one of the trails that I plan to explore later. This is my 3rd year here so I have walked through these woods before, but not as much as I would like. It is quite lovely here."

"It is, I agree. That's what has brought me back here for 7 years now."

"I just can't believe we never met. But, different seasons, I understand. Well, I might have to switch my season if you continue to come here in the fall, Maisy. I wish we had met sooner."

"But we've met now."

"Yes. Shall we have dinner?" Mitchell offered Maisy his arm and they walked into the dining room, led by Robert, their waiter from afternoon tea. Always the gentleman, Mitchell pulled out the chair for Maisy to sit before Robert had a chance to do it. She stumbled slightly, grabbing Mitchell's quickly proffered arm to steady herself.

"Oops, are you ok?"

"Of course, I'm fine. My shoe caught on the carpet, that's all." Once she was seated, he sat in the chair closest to hers.

The dinner progressed as their tea had earlier that day, pleasant and engaging. They talked about books, of course, and about life in general. They had similar interests in nature and walking, both enjoying the great outdoors more than almost anything else, except maybe reading. Mitchell wanted to find out more about Maisy and her wants and needs and suddenly realized, he had asked her how she made a living and she had deflected the question by instead asking him about his novel. He decided she didn't want to tell him but to be sure, he made another attempt.

"So, do you work in a city? If you are like me, a place like Deep Lake House is even more precious since it serves as a soul cleansing after working in a city 5 days a week." And then he waited for her response.

"Yes, I do. But just 2 or 3 days a week. I mostly work at home."

"Oh, lucky you! How did you work that out?"

"Well, I read books. I'm an editor so I can read anywhere. I don't have to take the train to an office."

"Yes, that does make sense. May I ask what kinds of books you edit?"

"Sure. I edit poetry, of course, but also children's chapter books. I think when a child reads their first chapter book has to be one of the most exciting times in a child's life. Most authors who write them can point to a single book that they read as a child that set them on the path to becoming a writer, that influenced their decision to write. Children are so open to learning and there is always a lesson you can write about and with some beautiful illustrations, you have a book. But a chapter book is now stretching their minds because they have several characters doing different things and they need to remember these from one chapter to the next. And there is often a moral to the story, another lesson, but it is more complex than a simple children's picture book."

"So is that what you read when you come here. I saw the pile you had at tea."

"A few, but vacation is also a time for me to read more grown-up books, too."

"That sounds like a job made in heaven, especially for an editor. How long have you worked there? And also, when do you think you'll publish your own book of poems?"

"I guess it is my turn to share something about myself." And Maisy laughed although she really didn't know too much about Mitchell. Mitchell loved her laugh and couldn't help but laugh along with her.

"Only reveal as much about yourself as you are comfortable with, Maisy. Writers tend to put their noses where they don't belong or push too hard to try to force people to share their deepest darkest secrets. So, forgive me if you feel as if that is what I am doing and know that it is only in the name of literature that I'm asking such personal questions."

"I understand. Although I do read a lot of children's books, I also read a lot of poetry and have found that the authors of these poems must have experienced great passion in their lives or they somehow persuaded others to share with them a love that they lost or one that ended tragically or even one that was unrequited. But that is often how love ends. It seems more likely to end in tragedy than continuing to grow. And sometimes that happens when one person is unfaithful and trust can never be restored if people are honest with themselves."

"Do you think that most great loves have to end somehow, that they couldn't continue to exist for these poets that you speak about? From what you just said, Maisy, it feels like there can be no great love that exists and lives on, there is only great love through some tragic ending: a death that happened through suffering or a life ended too soon, or that happened for only one person and from a distance, or when one person falls out of love with another. All very sad. Is there truly no happily-ever-after love? No love that lives on for 30, 40, or more years between two people? Although I haven't read a lot of poetry, I'm beginning to think I don't want to read any at all." Mitchell was suddenly losing his appetite for dinner. A sensitive man, he definitely believed in true love and thought of himself as a romantic and faithful man who would give his life for the woman he loved. He thought, since they seemed to have so much in common, that woman could be Maisy. But it seemed as if she didn't believe in true love at all. She must have lost a love and now only believed that love, with most people, was false somehow.

"Oh, I'm so sorry, Mitchell. I didn't mean to discourage you in any way. I'm sure there is a true and honest kind of love. I just haven't experienced it, personally, and I never read about it in the thousands of poems I've read over the years."

"Were you ever in love?" Mitchell knew he was pushing the boundaries over what was deeply personal but he wouldn't learn anything if he didn't ask. And Maisy might not even answer him.

"I was. It ended. Yes, tragically. He was unfaithful. Men do seem to wander more than women. Or they believe there is something, or someone, better just over the hill, or next door, or the next woman they meet on the train. Or they return to an old love and realize she was the one he was truly in love with, until they meet the next woman. So, not something I…" And just like that she stopped talking.

"Oh Maisy, I'm so sorry. I didn't mean to bring up sad memories for you. I just, I want to know more, everything, about you."

"It's fine, Mitchell. Yes, they are sad memories, in a way that I spent a good four years of my life with a man who I thought was my everything to find out he was cheating all along. Those long business trips, you know, and I was so naïve, I believed he was my one and only love. But, also anger, at myself mostly, that I believed him, that I didn't know the signs." Maisy wiped away a tear. Mitchell reached out for her hand, which she pulled back. He wanted to hold her, hug her, assure her that he would never treat her with anything but great respect.

"But how could you have known? Please don't be angry at yourself. I understand how men can be. I work with one, in particular, who has bragged to me about the woman he visits every couple of months by finding a reason to take a trip. I want to tell Personnel that he is going on this trip, not just to see a client but also his mistress, and I want to tell his wife who is home with their two children waiting for him to return. This man was my friend until he started confiding in me, probably to alleviate his own guilt about cheating, you know, telling someone what he was doing. Now when he wants to go for a drink or invites me to dinner, I find excuses not to go. I think he is the lowest form of human being and I want nothing to do with him." Mitchell felt the anger rising in him as he thought about his co-worker. He wanted this dinner with Maisy to be perfect and now they were both upset. This was not how he imagined their dinner would go. He wished he could do this night over again.

"Maisy, I'm so sorry I brought all this up. This was not how I imagined our night would go. Please, can we do this over, tomorrow night?"

Maisy seemed lost in her thoughts again and Mitchell once more reached for her hand. This time she put it on the table and let him hold it, taking it in both of his hands. He wanted to kiss her hand but thought that might be a bit too forward.

"Why don't we just continue with this night and order our meals." He hoped that didn't mean she wasn't interested in having another dinner with him. He reluctantly let her hand go and reached for his menu.

Their meals, thankfully, were a success with each ordering the same dish, trout with olives and tomatoes, a side of green beans, and a baked potato. Mitchell cleaned his plate and Maisy ate almost half of her meal. Both refused dessert but ordered tea.

They remained quiet after the meal, passing comments related to the meal and the excellent cook. Mitchell was concerned about asking any more personal questions and waited for Maisy to direct the conversation. After their tea came and they were both settled in to relax while digesting their meal, Maisy began to talk about a book she was currently reading.

Mitchell silently gave a sigh of relief since he didn't want their evening to end on their last topic which had caused Maisy such distress. His favorite subjects, of course, were reading and sharing his writing, too.

"I haven't read a lot of science fiction but this one, Fahrenheit 451, just struck me. Another editor in my office explained to me how this affected her life and highly recommended that I read it. It was a frightening concept with the threat of book-burning the same as there had been in Germany during Hitler's time. And removing books if they contained certain subjects. And of course, since I'm in this business, I had to read this and found I couldn't put the book down. Have you read it, Mitchell?"

"Yes, of course, and I agree. Book burning has always terrified me because it is about control and people not wanting others to learn certain things that are written about in novels. If they can keep them from reading certain ideas then maybe they won't want to change the way things are now. Very frightening."

The evening progressed and when they both realized they were the last two in the room and Robert was still waiting for them, they decided it was time to end their evening. Mitchell had the meal charged to his room, despite Maisy's suggestion that they split the meal.

"You can get the next one." Mitchell laughed, knowing he was not about to let Maisy pay for her meal the next time they ate together. And he hoped there would be a next time.

As Mitchell walked Maisy back to her room, he thought it might be a good time to give Maisy a good-night kiss. He was quite taken with her as well as very attracted to her. He knew wanting anything more was out of the question, and he had only the utmost respect for Maisy and wouldn't even consider, at this early time in their relationship, anything more than a kiss on the cheek. At least he hoped he could give her that. And if that didn't work out, he would at least kiss her hand. He was sure that would be acceptable. And before too much time passed, he wanted to be sure he got her address. Wherever she lived, he was willing to move to be closer to her. He had enough money saved that he could live off it for a few years, if he was conservative in his spending, which he was used to doing anyway. He was willing to give up everything for Maisy. He only hoped she felt the same about him.

When they reached her room, she had her key ready and quickly unlocked the door. She turned back to Mitchell, and without hesitating, Mitchell reached for her hand. That warm hug feeling surrounded her again and she smiled.

"Thank you so much Mitchell for the most enjoyable evening." Maisy blushed a lovely shade that complimented her russet-colored hair. Mitchell felt himself heating up and raised Maisy's hand to his lips, waiting for her reaction. She smiled, which he took as a sign of encouragement and leaned in to kiss her cheek but she, surprising him, turned her mouth to his. He was pleasantly surprised and moved in to put his arm around her while still holding her hand. They remained for mere seconds in this close embrace that felt like a place he wanted to spend the rest of his life. She pulled back and, although he wanted to stay where he was, he respected her wish and reluctantly dropped his arm while still holding her hand.

"Maisy, I..."

"Thank you, again, Mitchell." And just like that she was gone having slowly backed into her room closing the door. Mitchell stood, waiting for her to open the door again, to come back into his arms. And this time, he wouldn't let her go. He never wanted to let her go. He wanted her, only her. Miss Maisy Tuttle, the woman who, in the blink of an eye, had stolen his heart. He waited. And waited. And then he left.

The next morning Mitchell could barely wait to call on Maisy again, shaving and cleaning himself up to look presentable. He wasn't quite sure what his plan was but he couldn't let her get away from him. He needed to have a way to contact her and so he would start with that. He would ask for her address and then he would start making a plan to either move his job to where she lived or he would quit his job and find another job in her town. He knew he had valuable skills as an engineer and wasn't worried about supporting himself. He also had ample savings but he preferred not to touch that money so he could have a significant downpayment for a house. He wanted Maisy to have the best of everything and was sure a home would give her a sense of security so that if she wanted to leave her job and have children, or to complete her own book of poems, she could do it without financial worries. He just wanted her in his life. Forever.

Mitchell knocked quietly on Maisy's door so as not to wake her if she wanted to sleep in that morning. They'd had a very intense night, entirely due to his personal questions, which he deeply regretted. He wanted to make amends with Maisy before he did anything else. He listened at the door but heard nothing inside. He suddenly realized, it being 8:30, she was probably already at breakfast, perhaps waiting for him. He rushed to the dining room and, quickly scanning the occupied tables, did not see Maisy. He then walked to the front desk where he found James doing paperwork.

"James, good morning."

"Oh, hello Mitchell, is everything ok? Can I help you with something?"

"Yes, fine, I'm fine. But I was wondering, would you happen to know where Miss Maisy Tuttle is? I knocked on her door and there was no answer. I thought maybe she was at breakfast but she is not there. Did she perhaps go for a walk, maybe that's it. I could look for her on the trail around the lake."

"No, no, Mitchell, I'm sorry, you won't find her there. I'm sorry to tell you she checked out early this morning."

"This morning? But how is that possible? We had a wonderful dinner last night and now, she's gone? That can't be. She can't have gone far. If I leave now, I might be able to catch her."

"I'm afraid that is impossible. She left at around 6am."

"6am? But why, why would she leave so early? It's me, she was running from me."

"Running from you? But why?"

"I don't know, but I need to find out. I think we were getting too close and she was afraid. You see, she had a bad experience with a man that upset her and we discussed it. I was just trying to get to know her and now I've ruined everything. Her address. You must have her address."

"Yes, I do. But, we don't typically give out any personal information about another guest. I really don't think I should."

"James, you must, just this once. If Vera was here, she would tell you I have only the best intentions. You see, I'm in love with Miss Maisy Tuttle and want to marry her."

"Well, perhaps I can make an exception."

"Thank you so much." James left the front desk and went to the back office to retrieve information about all the guests. He soon came out with a piece of paper and handed it to Mitchell.

"Here is the address information I have for her. But I think she mentioned something about moving so I hope you can reach her. And good luck, Mitchell."

"Thank you, James."

Back in his room, Mitchell wrote a heartfelt letter to Maisy, proclaiming his love for her and asking if he could visit her. He didn't want to wait another day, another minute, of not being with her. He mailed it as soon as possible and spent the rest of his vacation trying to work on his book. His thoughts were not organized and he felt scattered and distracted. He decided to end his vacation early and after clearing his head by taking one more long walk on the Deep Lake property, he left for home.

The following year was Vera's last year as she had completed James' training. Her plan was to join her son and his family in Sweden and she was counting the days before she could leave. Even though she would miss her Deep Lake House family, she was ready to spend a much-deserved life enjoying her family and returning to her roots. She was sure her husband would have approved.

When Mitchell entered the front doors of Deep Lake House, he appeared to be a man so unlike the one Vera had the pleasure of meeting when he'd first arrived several years ago that she almost didn't recognize him as he made his way to the front desk.

"Mitchell, so nice to see you again. But you are not the Mitchell I remember, what has happened to change your demeanor so? You appear to be a man with a heavy heart, is there anything I can do?"

"How I wish there was. You were away last year when I came and I met Maisy Tuttle. Well, we hit it off and I… I fell in love, Vera. And then she left and I've searched for her since with no luck. My heart is broken. I thought she felt the same but it seems she did not and now I have no hope. I'm here this year in the hopes that we might meet again and I can find out what happened. But I know it is wishful thinking. If there is any way you could help me with this, I would be forever indebted to you."

Vera felt his pain and knew there was no easy way to tell Mitchell what she knew.

"I'm so sorry for your pain, Mitchell. But you must know. It wasn't anything you did and I have no doubt Maisy felt the same for you as you felt for her. But you see, she wasn't completely honest with you. She had a secret that it seems she thought was better not to tell you and chose instead to just disappear. Maisy Tuttle had cancer and passed away just a few months ago. I'm so sorry, Mitchell."

Mitchell wasn't sure he'd heard what Vera had just said and after asking her to repeat it, he turned away and finding a seat in the entrance hall, sat down. Vera stayed close to him, wanting to comfort the young man. She realized that with this news she'd surely broken his heart. She wished she could somehow reassure him with the usual expressions of sympathy for his loss, 'time heals all wounds', 'it is better to have loved and lost than to have never loved at all', but she knew none of these platitudes would comfort Mitchell. Instead, she sat quietly beside him waiting for him to speak.

"I could have helped her. I could have supported her, maybe find better doctors, ones who could have cured her. There are new treatments for cancer all the time. Why didn't she let me help her?" Mitchell shared his story with Vera and what he'd done to try to find Maisy. She'd been so evasive in giving out too many details about herself. Mitchell was so sure they would be together, he thought he'd have had time to ask for her address, her phone number, or any way to keep in touch. But then, without a word, she'd left before he'd had a chance to even ask her.

"What I do know, but I'm not sure now this will help you, Mitchell, is that she'd been fighting the cancer for some time. All the doctors had told her there was nothing more they could do. Please do not blame yourself for anything, Mitchell. But you may have some solace in knowing that you gave her what she needed more than anything. You gave her a reason to live, as long as she did, which was probably longer than the doctors predicted, because she knew she was loved. Even for the short time that you knew her. You gave her what not everyone gets in this life. You gave her your heart. You should be proud. And I am so happy she met you. You are a special man, Mitchell."

At that moment Mitchell realized that he had also been given a special gift. For a short time, he knew Maisy. For a short time, he loved Maisy. And now he knew why he met her. Why all those times they were both coming to Deep Lake House at different times, this one time they came at the same time because they were supposed to meet. Because they both needed what they both got. They were both truly loved.

Joanne and Drake

(1970s)

Chapter 9

The years of free love were a time of great romance paired with casual sex, loud music, hallucinogenic drugs, and unusual and mostly dangerous stunts. The 1970s, after just barely surviving the 1960s, opened the door to more freedoms than a young person had ever had the opportunity to witness much less participate in. And participate they did! The House certainly was not off-limits to the parties that lasted not just all night but all weekend long. Quiet time finally occurred when so many, who were drunk or drugged, simply passed out from too much of everything all at the same time.

One couple, Joanne and Drake Kersky, were originally paired with two other young people but soon found each other at one of the all-weekend bashes. Both in casual relationships at the time, they quickly became exclusive, spending long hours gazing deeply into each other's eyes. Young love always has the appearance of deep, true love but rarely has the stamina needed to make it to the 10-, 20-, or 30-year anniversary. I had high hopes for this couple; they truly seemed to like each other, had fun when they were together, and showed an acceptable amount of respect for each other.

Like most young married couples, the Kersky's spent most of their time in their room. Once they separated themselves from the party crowd, they were determined to appear as a civilized and professional young couple. Drake was a stock broker, Joanne a high school teacher, and they lived in the suburbs in a split-level ranch. They also planned to spend their two-week vacation every year at Deep Lake House.

Their first year at the House, away from old friends and hard-parties, was for their honeymoon. They came at a time when they were sure none of their regular crowd would be at the House. They didn't socialize much with the other guests, preferring their own company. On the beach they continued what one could imagine was their chosen activity in the bedroom; a lot of kissing and near naked closeness since they were both clad only in skimpy swimsuits. Pulling themselves apart when other guests would approach, they usually found a mostly secluded spot away from the main sunbathing area. But as I said, this was the first year. As with everything in life, change happens. And for many couples, change is often in opposite directions.

A couple, as they age, often become a wiser, more wrinkled, version of their younger selves. They are, for the most part, happier with who they are now and are able to accept the decisions they've made in life, despite the path they've taken to get there. And if they are lucky, they still love each other.

But some couples cannot endure change and as they age only become angry and disappointed with the life they now live, realizing, too late, that it wasn't the path they wanted to follow at all. Some fall out of love, some divorce, and some just settle for what their lives have become and die bitter and lonely. They've lost track of who they were and what was once so important to them. They long for the simple pleasures that once filled their lives and it seems they can no longer move forward. They give up trying. They give up living.

Joanne and Drake were sure their love would last until eternity. They lived only for each other, to be together, to love and be loved. At least they did that first year, on their honeymoon. But if you paid close attention to the two, who were so in love, you saw a weakening happening right before your eyes. It started one day on the beach. Drake had gone off to get them lunch at the House and while he was gone, a stranger wandered over to Joanne who lay face down tanning herself. Although they had taken their usual and mostly secluded spot, this stranger, a young man who was also staying at the House, had been exploring the lake and the surrounding woods.

"Hello. Sorry to bother you but I was wondering if you've taken any of the trails through these woods and if you could tell me if they lead anywhere or if I'd be walking for hours, and getting lost." Joanne sat up when the young man squatted down about 5 feet from her blanket. A handsome man with deep blue eyes and a smile that could charm any woman, Joanne felt a blush reddening her cheeks. She smiled back, flipped her long blonde hair over her shoulder and taking off her sunglasses, gave the young man a long look at her perfect facial features.

"Oh, no problem, I was just waiting… well, you see, no I haven't walked through these woods yet. We… I just got here a few days ago myself and haven't done much exploring yet. Sorry I can't help you."

"So, are you alone? Would you like some company? I don't imagine you're up for a walk." The man was very attractive and so physically fit that Joanne couldn't stop looking him up and down, flirting and smiling, posing to show off her bikini bathing suit.

She laughed, throwing her head back.

"No, not up for a walk. Just relaxing at the beach here. But sure, I suppose you could sit for a while before you start your walk." And she scooted over making space for the stranger on her blanket. The man sat and extending a hand, introduced himself.

"Brandon, Brandon Silvan. Pleased to make your acquaintance."

"Joanne, uh, Kersky." Brandon took her hand and, bringing it to his lips, kissed it softly. Joanne blushed and giggled, flattered by this gesture and his attention.

"So, are you staying here long at Deep Lake House?" She wanted him to stay and talk with her. She continued smiling and kept changing her pose, hoping to encourage him to spend more time with her. She thought about her life before Drake, she would probably be making out with this man by now if she hadn't married Drake. Drake. He would be coming back soon. She was so used to her 'free love' ways that it took her a few minutes to remind herself that she was married now. She wondered if Drake would ever consider having an open marriage. They'd never talked about it but, looking at Brandon, she would definitely consider it. She decided to continue flirting, wondering if it would lead to anything.

"I'll be here just for this week. Perfect amount of time, I would think, to have an unplanned but erotic kind of vacation. Don't you agree?" He was definitely flirting back. Joanne couldn't resist and moved a little closer. Brandon reached for her and, touching her long blonde hair, pushed a strand that had fallen forward behind her ear. She closed her eyes and tilted her head back just a little, waiting for him to kiss her.

"Excuse me, can I help you?" Drake was standing over them, holding a bag with their sandwiches and drinks. Brandon jumped up, surprised by this sudden intrusion.

"I was just talking to this young woman. Why? Who are you?"

"I'm her husband, that's who." Drake glared at the young man, waiting for him to leave.

"Well, she certainly didn't give me the impression that she had a husband. Good luck, pal." And Brandon walked away.

Drake stared down at Joanne who was checking her reflection in a mirror.

"Why do you have to be so possessive? I was just talking to him. He was going for a hike and wanted to know if I had hiked around here. That's all."

"Oh, that's all? That's all! If I hadn't come back when I did, I can't imagine what position I would have found you two in!"

"Oh Drake, you are being so dramatic. We were just talking. Brandon just got here a couple of minutes ago. And nothing was going to happen. Come on, babe, let's not spoil this beautiful day. What did you get us to eat?"

Drake couldn't settle down. He loved Joanne so much and couldn't stand having another man even looking at her. But this man, this stranger, had been touching her hair. And Joanne's eyes were closed, like she was waiting, just waiting, for him to kiss her.

"So, Brandon? You know the guy's name in just a few minutes of talking to him? Did you make plans to get together for later, maybe while I'm sleeping tonight?" He could feel his temper rising, jealousy taking over his whole body. Even though he had just sat down on the blanket, he couldn't relax and got up and started pacing, walking in the direction Brandon had gone.

"Drake, please sit down and let's eat this nice lunch you bought us. And, please stop this craziness. You have to stop this obsessive jealousy. I can't deal with it." Now Joanne was getting upset. She knew she had to get Drake out of this mindset or he would ruin their entire honeymoon. Everything had been going great. All she did was flirt a little, no harm done. But Drake always had to imagine the absolute worst. He was never like this before – when did he change? It had to be since they'd married. She wasn't his until she'd signed the marriage certificate and said the words 'I do.' Now he acted like he owned her. Well, Joanne wasn't having any of it. She had to put a stop to this, and pronto. She was always going to flirt and Drake just had to accept it, otherwise their marriage would end before it even got started. She loved Drake, but seeing him behave like this made it impossible for her to feel anything but anger and resentment. She felt like she was married to a child who had a new toy and wouldn't let anyone else play with it because all he thought was 'it's mine, all mine!' She had to let him know that under no conditions did she 'belong' to him in that way.

Reluctantly, Drake sat on the blanket again and reached for Joanne, who pulled away from him.

"Drake, you really have to stop this behavior. It's ugly and I don't like it. I've never seen this side of you before."

"You weren't mine before. And now that you are, I'll do everything in my power to keep you. And that includes keeping strange men away from you. Don't you know how crazy about you I am?"

Joanne jumped up from the blanket, it was her turn to pace now.

"You do not own me, Drake. I am not a piece of property that you bought. And if you keep talking like this, well, this marriage is not going to work for me. Brandon was just talking to me, keeping me company while you were gone. I thought you were going to hit the guy. Loving me is one thing but obsessing over me is something else. And I don't like it. I think we should be able to see other people."

"What? What do you mean, 'see other people'? Like date others? But we're married now, we don't date anymore. It's just you and me. And I'm not sharing you with anyone. How can you even suggest that?"

"I knew you'd be closed to that idea. You know, having an open marriage. A lot of people are doing it. You've heard about the parties, people in our neighborhood have them, you put your keys in a bowl and whoever's keys you get at the end of the night, that's who you go home with. It's a way to keep it in the neighborhood. No one gets hurt, you just have a good time that one night and then you go back to your spouse. But I imagine you would never go for that. You are so straight-laced. I thought you were more adventurous."

"I'm adventurous, with you, but not with our neighbors. And you're right, I'm not interested in swapping you with one of our neighbors. Besides, I'm not interested in any of them. I just want you. And it makes me absolutely crazy to think about another man having sex with you."

"So, you don't think Peggy's pretty?"

"Compared to you, no. Why would I want second-best when I've got the best. I'm not interested, end of discussion."

Joanne was right. She knew he wouldn't go for it. She found a couple of their neighbors quite attractive, like Peggy's husband, Randy. She would love to spend a night with him. And then of course there was Brandon, who she'd just met, who seemed ready and willing. She didn't know if her fantasies would be enough to serve her through their entire marriage. Even though they were only on their honeymoon, she was already feeling restless and wanted more adventure. What Drake didn't understand is that this could be the best thing for their marriage, would keep them interested in each other. Spending a night with someone just for sex and then going back to the man you love, what could be better than that?

"So, can we just eat lunch now. We'll discuss this another time. Let's just have our lunch and then we should probably take a nap, shower, and get ready for dinner. I would like to go down to the dining room tonight if you think you can stand to have other men look at me."

Drake suddenly pulled her to him and began kissing her face and neck. They both laughed. Joanne was delighted that Drake's foul mood was evaporating.

"Whatever you want. I would prefer to stay in the room and be alone with you. And if we get hungry for food, order room service. But right now, I'm just hungry for you." They kissed until another couple stumbled upon their secluded spot. It was time to find a new secret place.

Back in their room, after an hour of love-making followed by a brief nap, Joanne woke before Drake and hopped into the shower. She quickly got dressed and made herself up. Her reasoning was that if Drake woke and found her already dressed and ready to go to dinner, he wouldn't complain and would shower and dress to go downstairs, too. She didn't want to take all of their meals in the bedroom, she needed to get out of the room and she liked dressing up for dinner. But that wasn't how it worked out. Drake woke and was surprised to find Joanne all dressed up.

"What are you doing? I thought we were eating in the room? Are you hoping to find Brandon downstairs? Did you make plans to have dinner with him tonight?"

"Drake, stop! You can't keep doing this. You are going to split us up before we even have a chance to make a go of it. So, why don't you shower and then get dressed so we can go to dinner. Please! I'll go get some ice so we can have champagne later, ok?"

Obediently, Drake got off the bed and went to the bathroom, slamming the door behind him. Restless and irritated, Joanne left to find ice for the champagne they'd brought with them. It didn't seem like the best night for celebrating with champagne since Drake seemed to be only in a fighting mood. But maybe the champagne would help mellow him out. On her way to the kitchen for ice, the door to the room two doors down from theirs opened and Brandon came out, obviously dressed for dinner.

"Oh, hi again." Joanne gave him her most winning and seductive smile. Brandon stopped and smiling back, slowly closed the door behind him.

"Well, hello to you. Are you going to dinner, alone?" He glanced over her shoulder as if looking for Drake.

"Yes, I mean no, I'm just going to get some ice."

"I see, it does seem as if your husband could use a little cooling off." They both smiled at that. Joanne was back to flirting, touching Brandon's arm and moving a little closer to him. He reached behind him and opening the door to his room, grabbed Joanne's arm and pulled her into his room, taking her into his arms while kicking the door closed behind him.

"What are you doing? I can't be in here. You have to let me go!" Joanne, although she wanted to kiss him, was a little afraid now. Brandon was a bit too forceful for her and she wanted to get out of his room.

"You are such a dick-tease, I know what you want. You want this as much as I do." And then he kissed her, forcing his tongue into her mouth. She kissed him back, feeling herself weaken and then, as he started unzipping his pants, she grabbed the door handle and swiftly opened the door and ran back to her room. Drake was still in the shower and she sat on the bed, trying to keep the tears from falling and ruining her mascara. She knew she was to blame, she'd flirted and he'd responded, as men usually do. She brought this on herself. She would never share this with Drake; he would only say 'I told you so'.

She opened her cosmetic bag and fishing out her mirror, dabbed at her eyes and reapplied her mascara. She heard the shower stop and knew Drake would soon be out of the bathroom. Looking at herself in the full-length mirror that was on the back of the bathroom door, she fluffed her hair and straightened out her dress. Then she realized she never got the ice. What would her excuse be for coming back with an empty ice bucket? And then Drake came out of the bathroom, drying his hair with a towel with another towel wrapped around his waist.

"Hello gorgeous. So, where's the ice, I thought you would have the champagne ready and waiting for me when I came out?"

"No, I thought we could just get a drink with dinner. I don't want to drink too much tonight."

"Ok, fine. Then let me get dressed and we can go down to dinner."

Joanne nodded agreement and got up to look out their window that overlooked the front entrance of the House with a view, off to the right, that led down to Deep Lake.

Their dinner was pleasant and mostly uneventful. A new waiter dropped a tray that only had a couple of salads on it and, luckily, no one was nearby or they'd have had salad dressing splashed on their clothes. He was very upset and another waiter helped him clean up the mess, reassuring him that it happened at least once to every waiter. Joanne stuck to her commitment to have only one drink. Drake was already on his third gin and tonic. Dinner was winding down, they both had passed on dessert, when Joanne felt a hand squeeze her left shoulder.

"So, did you ever get your bucket of ice? I hope I didn't interfere with a honeymoon champagne toast. But then again, you didn't seem to be in too big of a hurry to get back to your new husband, were you, sweetie? And I'm sure you won't forget my room number, in case you decide to pick up where we left off earlier tonight. I'll look forward to it." As Brandon walked away Drake was rising from his chair, ready to chase after the man who'd just insulted his wife by implying that they were involved in a romance behind his back. But before he could step away from the table, the man was gone. Drake then turned all his attention to his wife, who appeared as stunned as he was. But it was obvious that she'd had some kind of interaction with Brandon earlier since he knew about her going for ice. But she didn't get the ice and had covered with the excuse that she wanted to have a drink downstairs with dinner. Drake was paralyzed and after standing, unmoving, for more than a couple of minutes, a waiter finally came over to the table.

"Can I get you something, sir?"

"Check, please." And then Drake sat down, waiting for Joanne to speak.

"Well, what do you have to say, Joanne? Have you been seeing this man when, what, I'm in the shower, or sleeping at night? On our honeymoon?"

"No, Drake, no, the man is disgusting. I want nothing to do with him. I just flirted a little at the beach, that's all, and now, I don't know, he thinks I want him, I guess."

"Is that right? Well, do you, do you want Brandon. Again, on our honeymoon?"

The waiter brought the check and started to walk away but Drake grabbed him, looked at the check, and taking money from his wallet, threw it on the table while standing up and motioning for Joanne to do the same. He walked behind her and out of the dining room. They were silent as they walked up the stairs and to their room. Once in their room, Drake let his anger and frustration out like Joanne had never seen before. He yelled and stomped, seemingly driven mad by his jealousy. Joanne sat on the bed, mascara trails streaming down her face.

"How can you do this to me? I thought you loved me, that we loved each other. And ON OUR HONEYMOON, you are hell bent on what, having sex with a stranger? I've never been so humiliated in my life. How can you do this to me? Why are you doing this to us?" Joanne looked at the man who just 24 hours ago she'd promised to love and cherish. Although she thought about other men and how much fun it might be to have innocent affairs with the neighbors, she certainly wasn't interested in ending their marriage. She realized she should have told Drake what Brandon did, should have said it wasn't her fault, that he'd grabbed her when she was walking by his room on her way to get ice. If only she'd told him this little white lie, they could have avoided all of this. She'd never seen Drake so angry and it frightened her.

"You're scaring me, Drake."

"Good, I want you to see what I would be like if you really did cheat on me. Although, who knows you may have been cheating on me this whole time, even before our wedding. After all, we weren't married yet. But since we are still newlyweds, well, what's the difference. It's almost like you aren't really married still."

Drake grabbed the bottle of champagne and, popping the cork, took a big swallow.

"I thought we were going to have that together." Joanne whispered. She tried to reason with him but there would be no reasoning, she could see that right away.

"Oh, did you now, to celebrate this beautiful thing we have, this marriage, our honeymoon. Yes, isn't it wonderful." And Drake continued drinking from the bottle.

"Drake, you're drunk. You've already had 3 gin and tonics, and now the champagne. Our champagne. You'll make yourself sick."

"I don't care. I don't care if I get sick. My life is ruined, our life together is ruined. It's over before it even started. How did this happen, Joanne? How? Am I just not enough for you? We have great sex together, but it isn't enough for you? I'm not enough for you? Then why, why did you marry me?"

"Don't say those things. Nothing is ruined. You need to stop being so jealous. Nothing happened with Brandon. He was just saying those things to get under your skin."

"Brandon, that's right, Brandon. How did he know you were getting ice for our champagne? And then what happened, did you go to his room? What the hell happened between you two while I was in the shower? What the hell, Joanne?"

"Nothing, Drake, nothing happened! You want to know, I'll tell you. I didn't tell you because I knew you would be crazy. I was going down to get ice and I happened to pass his room which he was just coming out of. I stopped and we chatted, he asked if I was going to dinner and I said we were. And then, I don't know, he kissed me and he opened his door and pulled me into his room and pushed the door closed. And when he started to unzip his pants, I got really scared and pushed past him and out the door and back to our room. That's what happened. That's all. It was about 5 minutes, that's all. I was afraid to pass his room again so I never went to get the ice."

Drake continued to drink the champagne and Joanne could see the anger building up in him. He took another big swallow of the champagne and with one swift movement, threw the bottle against the door to their room, the shattered glass flying around. Joanne got off the bed and stood in the corner next to the window. She was suddenly terrified of the man she thought she knew and loved. He had become a jealous, raging monster. She needed to leave, now.

Joanne snatched up her purse, the car keys, and headed for the door, dodging around Drake who was now unsteady on his feet. He tried to grab her but missed.

"Where are you going, to Brandon?!"

"No, but I have to get away from you. I can't be in this room with you right now. You are frightening me."

"No, babe, please, don't leave. I'll go. Let me go. I'll pick up the glass and then I'll go. You can stay here. I'm sorry. I'm so sorry."

Joanne sat on the bed while Drake picked up the pieces of the broken champagne bottle.

"Just be careful and don't cut yourself."

"I will."

When he finished picking up most of the pieces, he took the car keys that Joanne had put on the dresser, and walked toward the door.

"Just be careful, I'll ask housekeeping to bring up the vacuum in the morning. But don't walk over here with your bare feet. There could be small pieces. Just be careful."

"I will."

"Ok, then, I'll go now. I'm sorry." He stood at the door waiting for a response. "See you in the morning." Still nothing from Joanne.

Drake turned back toward the door and quietly left the room.

Joanne, who had been holding in the tears from fear and heartache, broke down.

Surprising to Joanne, she slept soundly. Probably because she was physically and emotionally exhausted after everything that had happened last night. She sat up in bed, lost in her thoughts when there was a knock at the door. Remembering the broken glass that was still in the carpet, she put on her shoes before walking to the door to look through the peephole. It was Drake.

"What do you want Drake? I just woke up and I can't deal with you right now." She looked at the clock on the nightstand and saw that it was only 7:20am.

"I need to use the bathroom, and shower."

"I think a shower can wait. And don't they have a public bathroom off the dining room?"

She looked out the peephole again and saw him looking down at the floor, obviously thinking about what to say next.

"Yes, there is. Ok, I'll use that one. Do you want to go to breakfast with me or are you still thinking about last night and can't stand to be around me right now?"

It was as if Drake had read her mind. She really didn't want to see him, not until she was able to shower and get her thoughts together. She also had no idea what she was going to do but she knew she couldn't live with this kind of obsessive behavior. Protecting her from an enemy is fine, if she is actually in danger, but protecting her from an imaginary foe was something she just couldn't live with and would not tolerate. Maybe they just never should have married. When he knew she wasn't his completely, he was on his best behavior, forever in the wooing stage of their relationship. But now that he believed she 'belonged' to him, it was as if a switch had been flipped in his head and he turned into a German Shepherd trained to kill anyone who came near his property.

She decided to meet him, in a public place, the dining room would do, and then try to talk some sense into him. Now that they were married, she wanted a baby but would not be trapped like that with a man who couldn't control his rage. She had to know if he could do that or she was out of this marriage. There was so much she loved about Drake but she was beginning to find out a few things about him she just did not like.

"Drake? Are you still there?"

"Yes." His voice, quiet, small.

"We can meet for breakfast. I need to talk to you. And this is serious, ok?"

"Yes, thank you, Joanne, Jo Jo, my Jo Jo. So, I'll see you downstairs?"

Jo Jo, his special nickname for her which she'd always liked. He used this when he wanted to get a smile out of her, even while they were in the middle of a fight. And it would soften her because he gave her that name the first night they'd met when he was falling head over heels in love. She knew it meant he was in a good place.

She quickly showered and met Drake in the dining room, sitting alone at a table, a cup of coffee in front of him and a cup in front of Joanne's seat. His head was down as if deep in thought, and she noticed that he had cleaned himself up, as best he could, using the public restroom. She realized she did love him and truly wished they could work this crazy jealousy thing out. She was determined.

He stood up when she approached the table.

"Good morning, Jo Jo. How are you? Did you sleep well?" He was on his best behavior, just like when they were dating.

"I'm fine, yes, slept surprisingly well. And you? Did you sleep in the car?"

"I did. Yes. Exactly what I deserved. I'm so sorry, babe. I don't know what comes over me. Something just snaps in my head. I can't stand to see another man... any man... even look at you. I just start picturing him in bed with you and pleasuring you and you kissing him and I lose it. You know?"

His obsession with Joanne was disturbing to her and she felt as if maybe she'd made a mistake. She was beginning to feel that maybe it wasn't safe to be around Drake, especially when he was in a rage. He had never expressed these intense, jealous feelings before and if she had known, she most likely wouldn't have walked down the aisle with him. She didn't think she could handle this kind of obsessive love and realized she didn't want to. She just wanted a normal relationship where they loved each other, had a family, and grew old together. He seemed to be waiting for a response but she didn't know what to say to what he had just revealed to her. Should she let him know he frightened her, his unhealthy obsession with her? That might make everything worse. Why didn't she already know this about him? She wondered if therapy would even help – perhaps his behavior was based an old girlfriend who'd broken his heart? She wanted to feel hopeful and decided to suggest he talk to a professional.

"I don't understand your behavior, Drake. Not at all. I sometimes like to flirt a little. I think a lot of women do. We like to feel, even though we are married that we are still attractive."

"Are you kidding, you are gorgeous, you have to know… "

"Yes, I understand you are very attracted to me. I know that, Drake. I'm just saying, this is how many women think. To know that others find them attractive. Not that anything will happen between you and another man, but it just confirms that you've still got it, you know? I would think that you'd be thrilled knowing that another man finds me attractive, but that I'm with you. I married you. I'm not with them. And if we continue to love each other, we'll grow together, have a family together, and be together till the end. That's how I think."

"Wow, you are amazing. That's a fantastic way to look at it."

"I need you to talk to someone, Drake. To get this crazy jealousy thing out of your head and, like I said, realize how lucky you are that you get to sleep with me every night and love me and that I love you."

"I would do anything for you, Jo Jo. You know that. If you want me to talk to a shrink, I'll do it. But I love your way of thinking. If I can just keep my head there and not go to the dark place, I think I can work this out. But I also need you to maybe curb your flirting, just a little? That's how we work together, right?"

"Yes, you're right. I will. I know sometimes I try to make myself appear as if I'm single," and Joanne remembered the incident the day before with Brandon, knowing that if she hadn't made herself appear available, she most likely wouldn't have had to avoid his advances, "but this newlywed thing is so new and I'm used to being free to do as I wish with whatever man I find attractive." Drake visibly stiffened at this admission and Joanne reached across the table to touch his hand.

"But that was then, this is now. And like most relationships, we both have work to do. And we both have to work at it. Deal?"

Vegetable omelets with toast never tasted so good. Drake said it might have been the best breakfast he'd ever had, and Joanne smiled, feeling hopeful about their future together.

The Boydins

(1990s)

Chapter 10

As a wise Leo Tolstoy said, 'All happy families resemble one another, but each unhappy family is unhappy in its own way.' The Boydins were one of the rare happy families that I had the pleasure of meeting here at Deep Lake House. They brought only joy and happiness to the house. There was always laughter and smiling faces as they entered the front doors of Deep Lake House. The happiest of families throughout the years, even after their three children came along.

When the Boydins first came to stay, there were only the two of them. Newlyweds, they'd spent their honeymoon, as many couples have done, at Deep Lake House. But they were different. They'd certainly spent enough time alone in the bedroom, but they'd also participated in every sport that was available at the House, from hiking to waterskiing to swimming and fishing. They did it all, together. And laughing all the way.

They didn't need any company because they enjoyed each other's company so much, sharing stories, feelings, and intimate conversations while looking deep into each other's eyes. People talk about 'soulmates' and these two were the epitome of the word.

The Boydins, Barbara and Hugo, were the longest-lived family who came to Deep Lake House, first just the two of them and then bringing their children over the years. And then, as each of their three children had grown and married, even their grandchildren joined them at Deep Lake House. My favorite kind of family. The ones who have found exactly what they need at the House, coming back year after year to relive that special something that, if you had asked them, I'm sure they couldn't say exactly what it was because it was unique for each of them and, yet, every member of the Boyden family felt it. They couldn't stay away from the House, even when their youngest son had moved far from home for his job, married, and had two of his own children, he would still, as often as he could, make the trip to Deep Lake House to bask in the warmth and love that surrounded him while in the company of his parents, siblings, his own family, and the magic of Deep Lake House.

In the 1990s, even though Barbara and Hugo's three children had grown and their grand-children were all entering college, the children did their best to make it, at least for a weekend, while their parents were spending their two weeks at Deep Lake House. A few times Barbara and Hugo had even rented several rooms at the House for a month, accommodating each of their children's growing families. James, the youngest, had two girls, Jessica and Tanya; the oldest girl, Evelyn, had a boy, Christopher, and a girl Michelle, and their third and middle girl, Marisa, had one girl, Antonia. Each of their children had graduated with honors from their respective colleges and went on to have successful and rewarding careers. Evelyn was an environmental engineer, Marisa was teaching college English to students at her alma mater while working on her third novel and volunteer teaching English to third-world country students, and James was working on Wall Street as a stockbroker while also spending much of his time volunteering with the Red Cross on various committees to bring food and shelter to those in need. Barbara and Hugo couldn't be any prouder of each of their children. They knew they had taught them right.

And now this year, as planned, Barbara and Hugo had come for their regular vacation. Seniors both in their 80s and slowing down just a bit, they still got out to walk on the well-worn paths around Deep Lake House and canoe around the lake, stopping to eat their picnic lunches and then, sometimes, napping for a bit. Evelyn, Marisa, and James had all promised to come, bringing their spouses as well, since they'd all now retired and were enjoying their own free time off, although they each still volunteered in their communities. Barbara and Hugo were looking forward to seeing their children and, having reserved three rooms, one for each of them, awaited their arrival. Barbara and Hugo were also thrilled that the children would be staying for an entire week. Dinners out and a few special events had been planned. Although they'd all seen everything in the area at least a dozen times, none of them seemed to tire of making the same excursions as in years past and only focused on their joy in being together, enjoying each other's company and the conversations that often kept them up late and even into the early morning hours.

The day of the children's arrival was full of excitement, as usual, for Barbara and Hugo. They checked with Russell, the front desk manager, to be sure their rooms were all ready. Barbara especially was anxious and had asked for flowers to be placed in each of the rooms.

"Yes, Barbara, everything is in order. We picked fresh flowers from our own gardens just this morning. Please relax, everything is taken care of."

"And for dinner... "

"And your dinner reservations at 7 are all set – we brought in a variety of fresh fish and will have a vegetable lasagna."

"You know Marisa is a vegetarian, oh, yes, vegetable lasagna, perfect."

Russell smiled at Barbara; they'd gone through this scenario every year. He only wished his own parents could be as excited about his visits. You would think royalty was coming to visit and Russell envied the Boydins' children and how fortunate they were to have such amazing and loving parents as Barbara and Hugo.

"Did you find a nice cut of beef for Hugo? He does like a good prime rib, only occasionally now, you know. And I'll have a tuna steak, oh yes, you did mention a variety of fish, so, I guess we're all set?"

"Everything will be ready, exactly as you wish, Barbara. I'm here to ensure you and your family enjoy your stay."

"Oh Russell, what would we do without you?" And Barbara reached for his hands, squeezing them both in hers, which brought a tear to Russell's eye. Yes, the best parents ever.

Barbara could barely relax and spent a good part of the day in the lounge area, just off the entrance, waiting and ready to greet each of her children and their spouses when they arrived. She tried reading a book, but whenever the front door opened she'd look up to see who it was losing her place, and wound up reading the same few paragraphs over and over again. Hugo, who'd been sitting on the front porch reading his book, came looking for Barbara and found her with a cup of tea in the lounge area. And, of course, she looked up when he came in.

"Oh, here you are. Reading, are you?"

"Hardly. You know me. I'm so looking forward to our children arriving. I hope they all get here safely."

"Yes, my dear, I know you can't wait to see them. Neither can I. But just like waiting for a pot of water to boil, they won't get here any sooner by watching the front door and disturbing your own reading. They'll arrive when they arrive."

"I know, I know. The anticipation excites me and then, when they do walk through the front door, it's the greatest relief knowing they're finally here, safe and sound. Then I'll be able to relax and enjoy the week with them. But until that time, I'm all tied up in knots."

Hugo laughed and walked towards the dining room.

"Need a warm-up for your tea, my dear? I'm getting a tea for myself as well."

"Oh sure, although this one is mostly cold now. Maybe just another pot of hot water."

"I'll be right back." And Hugo continued on to the dining room.

It was just past the lunch crowd rush when the front door opened and in walked Marisa with Evelyn close behind while their husbands brought in their luggage. They were sharing a laugh and when Barbara saw them, she jumped up from her chair and rushed towards them. They both stood with open arms and the group hug, replete with tears, lasted for several minutes. The husbands waited their turn and then they hugged Barbara. Hugo, who was close behind Barbara, walked into his girls' waiting arms. And the handshakes with the two husbands turned into another group hug.

"Your mother has not been able to relax, waiting for you all to arrive. How is it you all came together?"

"We met at the airport. Our flights had the same arrival time, so we shared a car that Mathew had reserved. It was wonderful, we got to catch up on our ride here." Evelyn was smiling from ear to ear and wrapped her arm around her younger sister.

"Yes, we couldn't have planned it any better. But let's check in so we can sit and chat."

"Already done, you just need to pick up your keys." Barbara was so proud of herself for doing her best to make life easier for her girls.

"When do we expect James to arrive? Has anyone talked with him yet?" The only boy, and the youngest who was doted on by the entire family, James shone brightest when surrounded by his highly supportive and loving family.

"I talked with him this morning – he and Laura were on their way to the airport. His flight was a bit longer than either of ours so he might get here a little later. But let's get unpacked and then we can relax." As the oldest, Evelyn always made the right decision.

"We were waiting for you to have lunch, did you eat?" Barbara was hoping they hadn't so they could all sit and enjoy a meal together. And, of course, they would be having dinner in the dining room that night so perhaps just a light lunch would do.

"I could have a little something, nothing too heavy. You did make reservations for tonight, right dad?"

"Yes, we did, at 7pm I believe, right my dear?"

"Yes, at 7. I was thinking just something light for now. Most of the lunch crowd is finishing up, so we'll mostly have the dining room to ourselves."

"Sounds perfect, mom." And both Evelyn and Marisa hugged their mom again.

Half an hour later they all met in the dining room. Barbara and Hugo were already seated and had water set at each place with a seltzer and lemon for her and Hugo. They all perused the lighter fare items on the menu and she and Hugo decided to share a couple of stuffed mushrooms, one of their favorites at the Deep Lake House dining room. Evelyn and Mathew and Marisa and Stefan got a couple of variety plates, one with cheese and crackers and the other with spinach artichoke dip with pita bread. Barbara and Hugo were being brought up-to-date with all the news about their grandchildren and great-grandchildren when a voice at the entrance to the dining room caught them off guard.

"Can anyone join this group or is it all full up?" James and Laura walked towards the table as Barbara, Evelyn, and Marisa jumped up to greet James with yet another group embrace. Hugo also made his way to and joined in the lovefest. Stefan and Mathew stood and shook hands with James and gave a hug to Laura before they took their seats at the table.

"Where's your luggage?" Barbara just couldn't help herself; she was very good at organizing and wanted to be sure everyone was settled in their rooms and ready to spend a relaxing week together.

"We spied you all here in and decided to put our luggage in our room before joining you."

"Perfect! So, settle down, order some drinks, and let's hear about my granddaughters, Jessica and Tanya."

"Oh, please, let Evelyn and Marisa share first. I'm the youngest and was taught the older ones, because of seniority, go first. And, then I'll go last. Just trying to make things fair. Right, mom and dad?"

Evelyn and Marisa laughed, along with their parents. This was a private joke with all of them.

"Well, since we got here an hour or so ago, we've already filled mom and dad in on their other grandchildren and great grandchildren so now it's your turn."

There was so much to share among the group that not a second went by when someone wasn't talking. There was a lot of laughing and even a little crying when James and Laura shared the news of her mother's passing. Her father had died just a couple of years ago and her mother had come to live with James and Laura.

"She went in her sleep. I checked on her that morning, as she was usually the first up, and when she wasn't up yet, I knocked on her door and there was no answer. I knew something was wrong." Laura held back the tears as long as she could – it had been just a little over a month ago and still felt so recent. "That's why we couldn't miss coming here – you are my family now and I'm so happy I have all of you." Barbara couldn't hold it in any longer and had to go to Laura and give her a hug, joined by Evelyn and Marisa. James felt so grateful to have been born into this loving family.

After a while, and with still more hugs, they all departed and went back to their rooms to rest and freshen up before returning for dinner. Evelyn said she needed a nap so she and Mathew went to their room. Although Marisa wanted to stay with her parents, Stefan wanted a nap so they also went to their room. Barbara and Hugo were still wound up from the anticipation of and eventual arrival and presence of their children, but Barbara knew that if she and Hugo wanted to be awake at dinner, they had better take a nap as well. And before returning to their room, James and Laura decided to go for a quick walk in the woods which was one of their favorite things to do at Deep Lake House. There was time to relax and recharge and they all enjoyed the quiet of the House in the late afternoon.

In a few hours they were all rested, dressed, and ready for dinner. Their table was waiting for them and after the drinks arrived and they all toasted to another fabulous vacation at Deep Lake House, they ordered dinner. Once dinner selections were made, Evelyn said she had an announcement to make. Looking at both Marisa and James, who couldn't hold back their smiles, she then focused on Barbara and Hugo. They waited in anticipation for whatever news Evelyn was about to share.

"So, mom and dad, this is an extra special vacation and we all needed to be here to share a special announcement with you - once the decision had been made by all of us."

Barbara grabbed Hugo's hand, unsure of how to feel. There was so much mystery around what Evelyn had just said, she couldn't imagine what was coming.

"Anyway, Mathew and I just sold our house. It was time to downsize and since our children are spread all over the country and with Christopher living in Australia, we thought we might as well look for a house… closer to you both, mom and dad."

Barbara gasped, holding one hand to her chest and squeezing Hugo's hand with the other. At that point, Evelyn sat and Marisa stood up.

"We also just sold our house and are moving back to where you both live. We actually just found a house on your street. Now if that is too close, we can probably find one in the next town over, but I'm thinking you'll be ok with us living nearby."

Now Barbara was crying, both of her hands on her face, tears escaping from between her fingers. Hugo had his head down, leaning on his elbows, his hands on the sides of his face. Everyone knew, his shoulders shaking, that he was crying, also. And then James stood up, Laura grabbing his hand as he spoke, choking back his own tears.

"And now, your only son, your 'baby' is coming back to you, also. As long as I can bring my wife." And they all let out a much-needed laugh. "We've also sold our house, it's a good market out there right now, and we have two houses to look at right after our vacation here is over. So, what do you say mom and dad? We aren't really coming back to the womb as they say, but we'll be pretty damn close to it." Before they knew it, Barbara and Hugo were on their feet along with the entire table and everyone was hugging and kissing and crying. A few minutes later, after they'd gotten out all the happy tears, their salads arrived and they all sat back down.

"I can't tell you how happy this makes your dad and me. We've been talking about the possibility of selling our house and moving closer to one of you. But since you all live in different states, and we didn't know which of you we might bother the most with our complaining about the lawn needing mowing, or your dad not being able to go up on the ladder and clean the gutters, or any of the other problems we'd need help with, well, this is just the best news possible." She and Hugo hugged and began to cry again, holding each other as tight as they possibly could.

"And now you're going to have to eat your tear-drenched salads before our main meal comes, so let's dig in. I'm starving." James was always the best at lightening the mood.

Dinner passed pleasantly, even more so since they could all see how happy Barbara and Hugo were having all shared their exciting news. Dessert and coffee followed the meal mostly because none of them wanted to leave the table. They were all so thrilled with the decisions that they'd made and how they were all going to be back together again, and how this time it would be even better. Again, the dining room emptied out while they all continued to talk, laugh, and enjoy each other's company. Finally, Marisa yawned followed by Barbara and Hugo, who were the first to declare, reluctantly, that it was time for bed.

"As much as we'd love to stay up with you all until the wee hours of the morning, we need some sleep. This day has been more than we, your dad and I, could've possibly hoped for. We love you all so much and can't wait to see what our future together will hold."

"How about Alaska?" James had been talking with Laura about going and knew that his parents had also mentioned going to the great state.

Barbara felt another tear forming and shook her head at the love that poured out of her children and onto her and Hugo.

"Let's save something for tomorrow, shall we?" Evelyn gave James a look that said, don't tell them everything! Leave some surprises for later. James zipped his mouth and nodded in agreement.

They all got up from the table with Evelyn, Marisa, and James all approaching their waiter who'd been patiently waiting for the family to leave. They'd put aside a $150 tip to make up for any inconvenience to Paul, who'd waited on them while also tending to a couple of other tables in the dining room, and to thank him for his excellent service and let him know how grateful they were for his patience.

Paul was very appreciative of their generous tip and he thanked them multiple times as he began cleaning up their table. And finally, with that taken care of, off to bed the families all went.

There were no early risers the next morning, except for Hugo who was always the first up. He got his coffee and settled in on the front porch on one of the rockers. It was a beautiful morning and he loved watching the ducks and other birds fly in to the lake, enjoying the beauty of Deep Lake as much as Hugo did.

Shortly after, Barbara came down and found Evelyn and Mathew with Marisa and Stefan in the dining room, all sipping their coffee and enjoying each other's company.

"Has anyone seen your father?"

"No, Mathew and I came right to the dining room and Marisa and Stefan came down about five minutes later. No sign of James and Laura yet, either." Evelyn gave a quick look around the dining room, but there was no sign of Hugo.

"I'll go check out on the front porch. He sometimes likes to take his coffee out there. It's such a beautiful view. We should all go out there." Barbara turned towards the front door of the House in search of Hugo.

The group at the table continued their conversation when it was broken by a scream coming from the front of the House. They all jumped up, knowing it was their mother, just as James and Laura were making their way into the dining room.

"It's mom." They all ran to the front door and out onto the porch. There they saw Barbara, sitting on the porch at Hugo's feet, her arms wrapped around his legs, crying the tears of a woman whose heart has been broken in half. The children with their spouses ran to their mother and father, sitting in the rocking chair, with his head slumped forward on his chest. James ran back inside to alert the House that they needed an ambulance at once. Russell called immediately and James ran back outside to help in any way that he could.

"Please see if you can find a blanket, or a pillow, or something so we can lay him down. I fear he might slip out of the chair." Evelyn always knew what to do, even in an emergency. James and Laura ran inside together and after talking to Russell, he quickly recruited one of the bedroom maids to bring a pillow and blanket from storage. Back outside, the group had gathered together and laying their father on the porch, took the pillow and gently put it under his head and covered him with the blanket. For a group that had all the appearances of people suffering from shock, they all went about doing what needed to be done in a loving and efficient manner. Barbara sat next to Hugo on the porch, refusing to leave his side even though all of her children tried to get her up and have her sit in a chair.

"I've always been by his side, through these more than 60 years, I'm not going to leave him now." That seemed to break the spell and soon they were all crying.

The ambulance would bring Hugo to the local hospital but the EMTs, after taking his pulse, knew he was gone. They asked Barbara if she wanted them to try to resuscitate him, but since she was still in a state of shock, her children all spoke for her, agreeing that Hugo was gone and had most likely died more than an hour ago.

And so ended this vacation that all of the Boydin children had waited for to share their news of moving closer to Barbara and Hugo. The children did all find homes closer to Barbara, as they had planned, and the following year, they all made their way back to Deep Lake House. Barbara came that year, too, but she said it just didn't feel right without Hugo. She never came back. Her children made an attempt to recreate what they'd all loved about Deep Lake House by inviting their own children with their spouses and grandchildren, but it was never quite the same. And within a few years, none of the Boydins ever returned. What had made Deep Lake House special for them was how Hugo and Barbara had brought their family together in a fun and relaxing place. The magic they'd all experienced was gone once Hugo was gone. And Deep Lake House never had a more loving and enjoyable family than the Boydins.

Special Acknowledgements

Always, and foremost, I must thank my partner in life and in everything I do, Jim Fontaine. I can't imagine ever getting my books out in public without the professionalism and perfectionism of Jim's keen eye for details giving it not just a once over but as many times as it takes to make it the best possible book that it can be. You rock! Do I even have to mention the time, effort, and energy you've put into updating the website? An unpaid position, I know you did it for love!

I also wish to thank a few friends for their positive support of my work and feedback they have given me for all of my books that they've read, in particular Vivian Ward, Nancy Strout Porter, and Bonnie Anthony. I know I've said 'thanks' many times but it never seems like enough. Vivian, my 'oldest' friend (in years of friendship!) has been so supportive of my writing, even asking her son to buy two of my books for her Christmas present. Nancy, my writing buddy, has been most helpful in getting me to stay on track with my writing. I'm sure this book would still be in the 'almost done' stage if not for Nancy's suggestion to be accountable to each other. It worked! And of course, a special thank you to others who have supported my work by purchasing everything I've written (Natalie and Jim Kelley, in particular). I do and always will greatly appreciate you.

About the Author

DJ Geribo, author and fine artist, lives in rural New Hampshire near Lake Winnipesaukee. After pursuing fine art for many years, she decided to focus on her writing and has completed several children's books, 'Eddie Easel and the Case of the Missing Green', 'Mouse Bound', and a middle-grade book, 'The House at the Top of the Trees'. She has also written a non-fiction book about one of her dogs that contracted a life-threatening disease, 'The Miracle Dog'. Her more recent books include a collection of literary short stories in 'Seven Storied Houses', and a collection of memories compiled from childhood events in 'Me and Them'. 'The Mart' combines a novel with a related collection of stories. 'Deep Lake House' is her eighth book.

Besides writing, which keeps DJ very busy, she also enjoys reading, of course, painting, exercise in many forms from lifting weights, e-bike riding, golfing in the summer with her husband, snowshoeing in the winter months, and walking any time of year. She also loves just hanging out with her Pomeranian and her Cockatoo.

DJ's books can be purchased at any of the following: the author's website at www.DJGeribo.com, BBD Publishing's website at www.BBDPublishing.com and from Amazon where you can also purchase a few select titles in Kindle format.

To learn about her latest and forthcoming books, visit her website and join her e-mail list or visit BBD Publishing's website.

Other Books by DJ Geribo

The Mart: A novel and a collection of stories where the characters appear in both the novel and the stories. The two main characters dominate the novel but the characters all have their starring roles in the individual stories. Together they complement each other in a world that both lifts your spirits and breaks your heart.
Softcover - $17.95

Me & Them: A memoir like none you've ever read before. If you grew up during the 50's and 60's, you'll feel right at home in this collection of daily life events. Some will make you laugh while others may make you cry. But you won't leave this collection without reminiscing about your own childhood memories.
Softcover - $15.95

Seven Storied Houses: A house isn't always a good indication of the kind of life that is lived by the people who occupy it. A mansion doesn't mean a happy family, nor is a much-in-need-of-repair home indication of a life of misery. Both are full of memories and only the occupants can decide if they will be good or bad.
Softcover - $15.95

The Miracle Dog: When the author's dog, Kameko, collapsed into her arms one summer morning, she knew something was very wrong. A trip to the vet confirmed a life-threatening diagnosis with DJ's precious Pomeranian spending nearly a week in an ICU at an emergency vet hospital that included four blood transfusions. After many almost daily trips back to the hospital, finally a combination of medicine saw DJ's beloved Pom back on the road to recovery.
Softcover - $16.95

Mouse Bound: A story that came about after a mouse set up residence in the author's studio. After live-catching and driving the mouse to another location, she imagined the adventures he'd have experienced in returning to the best and only home he'd ever known, back in her studio.
Softcover - $10.95

Eddie Easel and the Case of the Missing Green: A creative children's story that teaches a child the basics of art and painting all through an engaging mystery. A story any child will love and one that may even start your child on an artistic career path.
Hardcover - $17.95 – Exclusively through BBD Publishing

*The House at the Top of the Tree*s: While riding their bikes, Nat and Devon spot a house that appears to be sitting at the top of a tree. Curiously, they find a way to get there and discover a world unlike anything they've ever known before, a place where all of their dreams come true. Is it safe to stay or should they return home to their hard-working single mom who does her best to support her children who mean the world to her?
Softcover – $16.95

Coming Soon!

Useful Pieces: Seth and Jill move into the rental house owned by the older couple who occupy the mansion that dwarfs their modest guest house. While Seth and Jill each pursue their own artistic interests, a series of unusual events occur causing the young couple to question the motives of their landlords. Are they friends? Foes? Or, is something else the root cause of the strange happenings?

Castle at the Bottom of the Sea: – the 2nd middle grade adventure book featuring Nat and Devon (from *House at the Top of the Trees*) that takes them to the shore and another exciting and surreal adventure.

My Neighbor, the Alien: – Jeff and his best friend Wilt are sure Jeff's neighbor is an alien. But what is he doing in their neighborhood? And how does he know their teacher from school? It seems the real learning has just begun for the two curious boys.

All of DJ's book can be purchased at www.BBDPublishing.com

Selected titles can be purchased on www.amazon.com in either paperback or Kindle editions.

Leave Us a Review

Did you like *"Deep Lake House"*? BBD Publishing would love to hear your thoughts on this and any of the other books by author DJ Geribo that you've read.

Visit www.BBDPublishing.com and on the home page, click on the 'Submit A Comment' button in the right-hand column to share your review about this or any other books by DJ Geribo.

If you purchased this book on Amazon, please leave an Amazon Review to help other readers find and enjoy DJ's books.

Thank you for your interest in DJ Geribo's books.